A Fae Is
Done

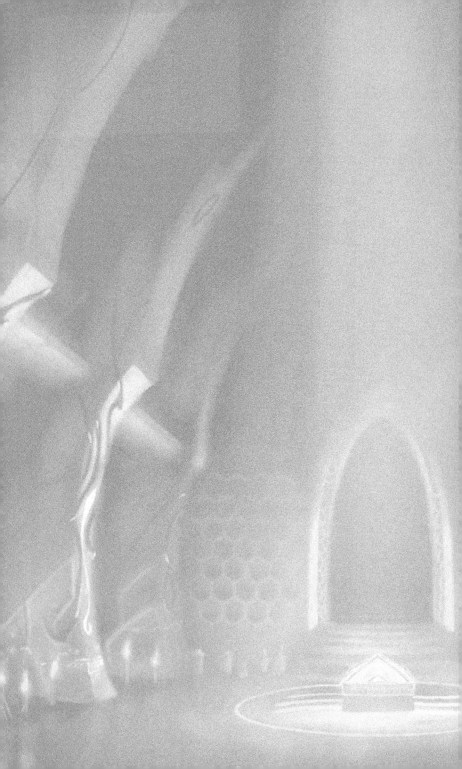

DANIELLE M. ORSINO

A Fae is Done

Birth of the Fae Book 5

4 Horsemen
Publications, Inc.

A Fae Is Done
Birth of the Fae: Vol 1 Book 5
Copyright © 2022 Danielle M. Orsino. All rights reserved.

4 Horsemen
Publications, Inc.

4 Horsemen Publications, Inc.
1497 Main St. Suite 169
Dunedin, FL 34698
4horsemenpublications.com
info@4horsemenpublications.com

Cover by Horsemen Publications, Inc.
Typesetting by Michelle Cline
Editor S. L. Vargas

Lady Danaus Photographer- Robert Milazzo
Hair and Makeup- Timothy Alan Beauty
Sunshine the carnivorous butterfly concept by: Danielle M. Orsino
Sunshine the carnivorous butterfly Illustration: PandiiVan
Crystal Catacomb: Lavillion
Map is illustrated by Daniel Hasenbos–he goes by Daniels Maps

Library of Congress Control Number: 2022941308

Print ISBN: 978-1-64450-659-2
Hardback ISBN: 978-1-64450-661-5
Ebook ISBN: 978-1-64450-660-8
Audiobook ISBN 978-1-64450-658-5

TABLE OF CONTENTS

DEDICATION

Thank you to each Fae-natic who has written me to say they have gotten lost in the Veil. Your words are the stars that light up the night sky and guide me on my journey. Here's to another adventure! Chaos be with us, and may we never stop dreaming, for the universe always has a way of answering. We just have to listen.

Valley of
Venis Grando

Will-o-Wisps

Oberon

Pixies

Dryad

Epican Forest

Salt Stream

Gerburah Rock Plains

Power Angel
Memorial

Ucca Statera

Bri

Fo

Crystal Causeway

Serena Bay

River Nimbue

Oaken Door

Merfolk

Court of Light

Na

A

Merfolk Garden

River Hope

Aubane

Sacred Grove

The
VEIL

ACKNOWLEDGEMENTS

PMD

Carlos & Penelope

Christina: Thank you.

4Horsemen: As always, it is a pleasure
to ride along with you.

Pandiivan: Thank you for your art.

PROLOGUE

O*h, kiddos, it's just getting good in the Veil. Betrayal, heartbreak, and death—who says entertainment is dead?*

I am thoroughly enjoying myself. These Fae are full of surprises. Let's recap, shall we? So far, Queen Aur—I am sorry, it's just Aurora *now. Aurora gave up the crown when she decided to play martyr and acted like she was going to murder her betrothed, the Dark Fae King Jarvok. This was all a ruse to keep him safe because her own bishops planned to kill her and frame him. Juicy! Oh, and she also gave up their child, but Jarvok doesn't even know she was pregnant.*

That's not even the best part. Aurora had her "friend" Lady Sekhmet perform a walk-in spell to transfer the unborn infant's essence into a dying human baby's body and then swept the baby off to be raised by humans. Yeah, that won't come back to bite anyone in the ass. Aurora wrote two notes to Jarvok, telling him where he could find their baby, and gave the notes to Sekhmet. I smell a devil in disguise, and they aren't doing a very good impersonation.

The information Aurora received about the betrayal came from Awynn—the dead bishop— in her dreams. Suspicious.

After Aurora staged the murder plot, it was revealed that (hold onto your hats, kiddos!) Awynn was a Shadow Kat, but no one knows who sent the creature after her. The Oracles and their Familiars exposed the Shadow Kat, but its information about the bishops' plot against Aurora was accurate. I always say, add a little truth to your lies; it's so much more convincing!

However, the damage was done. Aurora was tired of fighting and succumbed to her broken heart. Okay, it was by execution, but you get the picture. Poor Aurora would die never knowing which Fae had betrayed her—none other than her friend SEKHMET! The new Queen of the Court of Light. I may have the unwarranted reputation as the father of lies, but this was low even by my standards.

So, Aurora was executed, and now the Fae are on a new path.

Couldn't you just die!? *Well Aurora certainly did. What? Too soon?*

With this execution, King Jarvok, in all his hurt, has done me a gigantic favor. Something I thought I had lost so very long ago has been found. Mother Luna was correct: with death there is always a new beginning.

Chapter One:
WINGS

A urora was dead.

The first Queen of the Court of Light, the only Sylph, Guardian of Wind, the Virtue Angel known once upon a time as Xi, had met her Oblivion through her friend, the captain of the Royal Guard and founder of the Illuminasqua, Desdemona.

Captain Desdemona had fulfilled her orders and executed the disgraced queen for plotting to kill her betrothed, King Jarvok of the Court of Dark. Desdemona had used the notorious Harbinger swords, thrusting the blades through Aurora's heart, but Aurora, as though in one last act of defiance, had manifested her energy wings in a brilliant display of power. For a split-second, Desdemona had thought the fuchsia wings turned into golden feathers in recognition of their old angelic lineage, though this all seemed impossible, considering Aurora was wearing a black onyx choker to block any Magick. Desdemona couldn't be sure about the feathers, but she wasn't the only one to see the wings.

Bishop Geddes gasped at the sight and covered his mouth to hide his shock.

"She manifested *wings*! While she had the onyx collar on!" Bishop Ward exclaimed.

Geddes swiftly punched Ward in the gut. "Shut up, you fool, let no one hear you! You saw nothing," Geddes whispered as he pushed the shocked Fae toward Bishop Caer. "Get him together!"

Desdemona was not surprised by Aurora's demonstration; it was just like the former queen to defy convention. The captain pivoted, her swords held limply by her left hip, and announced to Bishop Geddes: "It is done." Some of the crowd wept; others cheered. The mix of reactions nauseated her.

Geddes looked down at the warrior Fae. "Captain, please demonstrate proof of your kill." To kill with a Harbinger sword meant the victim's essence would be transformed into a tattoo for the wielder of the sword to wear as a reminder of their kill.

Desdemona's grey eyes never left Geddes as she unbuttoned her vest, ripping at the fasteners, her fingers trembling, but she hid it well. The sounds of her breathing and the rustling fabric helped her to concentrate and not to cry. She had felt the familiar tinge of Magick; she knew where the Harbinger swords' trophy had made their home. She pulled the material of her vest aside, revealing the black tattoo she now bore over her heart. The marking read "Xi" in the old language of the Angels. It was Aurora's original angelic name; only those closest to the former queen would have known it.

For a moment, Bishop Geddes could not hide his surprise, but that was soon covered by a look of smug

justification. His nostrils flared and his goatee empha-
sized his smirk like a picture frame. "Thank you, Captain.
Your job is done. Guards, take the remains for cremation."
Geddes' white cape snapped as he pivoted to leave. Ward
and Caer followed, their faces emotionless, not an ounce
of remorse dripping from their auras. Only Caer glanced
back, but when he caught Desdemona's eyes, he looked
down and fell in line with the royal entourage. The new
queen had already been ushered inside, protected from this
charged debate. The bishops knew once the order for her
cremation had been given it would incite Aurora's loyalists.

"Wait!" Desdemona yelled as the Royal Guards
approached the stage. She fixed her eyes on the balcony,
holding the guards at bay with an outstretched hand. "She
was our queen. She is to be buried in the Crystal Catacombs
per her last wishes, not burned like a common—"

Jarvok stepped forward to the balcony, his hands
gripping the stone railing. "Like a common Power Angel,
Captain? You would have once been relegated to the pyre."
He leered, taking great pleasure in reminding Desdemona
where she had come from.

Desdemona was not ready to speak with him; she was
trying to keep her fury under control. It bubbled under
her skin. The swords were back in her hands, her grip
tightening as she pointed the blades skyward. He had
requested that she use the Harbinger swords on Aurora,
and as the intended murder victim, he'd had his request
granted. Desdemona would have relished impaling Jarvok
on her blades, watching the light dim from his eyes until
the demons came to claim him. *Hmm, nope, that won't
happen,* she thought glumly. *Not even Lucifer would want
Jarvok. The devil has better taste.*

"This is not your place, Jarvok," Desdemona called up to him. "You had your justice—leave us to handle this."

Up on the balcony, Asa touched her king's arm. "It is none of our concern what they do with her remains, my liege," she said softly.

The Dark Fae king stared at Desdemona a moment longer. "She played her part," he mumbled and pushed himself back from the railing.

Desdemona gestured with a Harbinger blade toward the gates, trying her best not to dishonor Aurora, because the desire to kill Jarvok was raging in her blood and she was barely hanging on, her knuckles matched the pearlescent hilt of her sword, "Aurora left her wishes to be laid to rest in the Crystal Catacombs. We must honor this." She turned her attention to Bishop Geddes. "Please, Bishop Geddes. Do not burn her."

"No! Take the body to the pyre." Geddes whipped his cape around, grandstanding as he exited the veranda. It was the equivalent of tossing a fireball into a room and closing the door.

The crowd whipped into a frenzy. Fae turned on Fae, pushing and shoving as they shouted their perspective on what to do with the remains. Many felt she was a traitor, and thus, Aurora's wishes were not to be honored. Some felt she was a hero for attempting to take Jarvok's life. They argued that the unification of the two courts was a bad idea. Others saw her as the downfall of the Court of Light, sullying their name by not honoring her word. A few Fae threw rotting fruit toward the veranda. Desdemona watched in horror as her kin dissolved into pandemonium.

Then two other players entered the arena with an air of triumph and nobility about them. Malascola, leader of the Spelaions, sat on the back of the white stag Theadova, the leader of the Aubane Faction. Theadova's gold-dusted antlers glittered in the light; the rose blossoms that had been small buds not long ago had bloomed. The magnificent sweetheart roses, in shades of pink and red, complemented his stark white fur. Malascola, with his iridescent green skin and beard, looked striking on the back of the oversized deer. The smaller Fae brandished a parchment.

"Aurora's final wishes were to be buried in the Crystal Catacombs that my kin made for her! I have Aurora's last words on this parchment. Honor them and turn her remains over to us," the leader of the Spelaions said. But without the bishops or any royal representatives to hear his evidence, anarchy set in.

Desdemona drew her other blade, knowing there was no one else to take control of the situation. Queen Sekhmet had been hurried along for the prophecy reading before Aurora's bleeding had even ceased. Bishop Geddes had run like the coward he was. She glanced at the burning blue torches. More Fae blood would stain the ground before this argument found resolution, of that she had no doubt. *The time for diplomacy has passed. These Fae need to be taught manners.* She was prepared to defend Aurora's remains, when pain rippled through her body, her chest seized, and her skin sizzled. While an uncontrollable mass of Fae tried to make their way to the platform, the pain dropped her to her knees. Clutching at her arm, she looked skyward in bewilderment.

Desdemona called out for the one person she trusted: "Nightshade!" In a heartbeat, the other Illuminasqua appeared. Nightshade removed her black hood. Her long, silken midnight hair was tied back in the exact same braid as her captain, and without her red-tipped bangs, she would have been Desdemona's mirror image.

"Captain, what can I do?" Nightshade knew better than to ask if Desdemona was hurt.

"Protect the body," Desdemona ordered through gritted teeth. Nightshade drew her own Harbinger blades and rushed to Aurora's body as her captain had commanded.

The commander of the Illuminasqua watched her protégé stand ready to confront boldly any Fae dumb enough to try for Aurora's remains.

A jolt of pain hit Desdemona again. Her back arched. As it passed, she dragged herself to the corner of the platform. The throbbing increased in intensity with each subsequent breath. A blue streak snaked up her right arm, originating from her Elestial Blade. The azure band infected her veins, and an explosion of colors overtook her arm. Desdemona unbuttoned her vest and ripped a strip of cloth from the bottom to act as a tourniquet, but it was too late. The streaks of color slammed into her heart. Her spine curved, and she threw her head back in pain. Her fists clenched and her Elestial Blade unsheathed on its own, glowing pink, a color she had never seen it emit. Her eyes unfocused, making the blade appear to shimmer. Then the throbbing ceased, leaving her limp, sweating, and breathing heavily.

The streaks receded from her heart. Desdemona looked down at the remarkable change to her body: the black tattoo that had read "Xi" not more than a few seconds earlier now glowed fuchsia, the same color as Aurora's energy wings, and in Fae lettering read "Queen Aurora." Desdemona sucked in a quick breath and covered up the new marking with her vest. She took inventory of her body. She felt fine; renewed, in fact. She was not sure of the how or the why, but she knew this meant something, and she would be damned if she let anyone touch Aurora's remains now.

Desdemona checked her back pouch for the ring she had promised to give Hogal. She had slipped it off Aurora when she inspected the queen's ropes. It was one of the first gifts he had made for Aurora as queen. It was a knuckle ring with a citrine crystal representing the sun, surrounded by triangular beams, and a crescent moon made of moonstone, pearlescent and delicate. Desdemona confirmed it wasn't damaged and put it away. She had given her word to Hogal that she would take care of him after Aurora's passing, and she planned to keep it. This ring was a symbol of her pledge.

The captain of the Illuminasqua drew her swords and charged forward. She would not let the Fae fall into anarchy; she would honor her oath, loyalty to her kin.

Chapter Two:
HIDE AND SEEK—OR JUST HIDE

E watched Indiga fly into the palace. He had agreed to play hide and seek, but now he was regretting it. Still, E chased after her through the small side door leading into the kitchen. He could hear Indiga giggling on her way up the winding steps. Nimbly, he avoided the large wooden island and vegetable baskets, and dipped his head low, trying to go unnoticed by the Fae tending to the bread ovens. E did not realize he was well past the kitchen and into the palace until he heard a sudden bang from outside. He jumped at the sound. "What was that?" He glanced around at the polished crystal walls and archways. E had never been inside the formal wing. Indiga knew the palace, though; she lived here. He slowed to a creeping walk.

"Indiga?" he whispered. "Come on, this isn't funny." E knew he was going to get in trouble. He listened for her, but she didn't respond. "Okay I'm leaving," he huffed, turning back the way he had come.

When he got to the end of the hallway, he couldn't recall if he had come from the right or left. *Was that statue*

there? He rubbed his head. "Indiga?" E called her name a little louder, but she didn't answer. Then he heard voices coming from inside a room. The door opened, and E hurried behind the statue as two tall, slim Fae walked out of the room. "The Oracles," he said under his breath. Their beauty and power were unparalleled. They walked side by side, two strangely ethereal carbon copies. They wiped at their eyes, and E watched them glide down the corridor until they disappeared around the corner. *They're crying? Oh no, Queen Aurora! I have to get back to my mom!*

E had carefully stepped out from behind the statue when he heard the clinking of spears on the quartz. "Royal Guards!" he exclaimed before slapping his hand over his mouth. E ran into the open room the Oracles had just come from. He shut the door and waited for the guards to walk past, but instead, they discussed taking watch at the door. E looked around frantically. *The Oracles will come back and find me here. Maybe the windows?* He threw them open to find a balcony. *Great! I'll just climb down.* He stepped out onto the terrace, just as a huge shadow eclipsed the sun. The little Fae looked up to see a dragon circling the balcony. The creature was yellow with blue and green feathers decorating its head, its large black tail fading into the striking yellow. It was a younger Acid-Breather. E froze, trembling, until the dragon flew out of sight. Then he ran back into the room and squeezed himself into the space between a chair and a triangular bookcase. It was a tight fit, but E was small enough to jam himself in without being seen. He tried to control his breathing and the tears beginning to sting his eyes. He wanted to go home.

The door opened, and the two Oracles walked back into the room. E was trapped.

Chapter Three:
OBSERVERS

R owan and Holly walked into the Contemplation
Room, now called the Reading Room, and after a
few moments, heard a commotion outside the doors.

"What is going on?" Holly asked the Oracles. She
gestured for Rowan to investigate as the muffled voices
became louder.

Rowan peered out.

There was a heated exchange between the Royal Guards
Rowan had seen when he and Holly walked in just a little
while ago, and two Hathor guards. The Hathor guards
insisted the Royal Guards were needed elsewhere. The
Royal Guards were leaving, as instructed, but not before
making it clear they were not happy.

Once the Royal Guards turned the corner and the
Hathor guards were alone outside the Reading Room,
the atmosphere changed. The Hathor guards wore gold
breastplates, and gauntlets with inlaid sequoia trees decorated their wrists—much more ostentatious than Aurora's
Royal Guard. Several bladed weapons hung from their

hips. These guards were not here for show; they may have worn brazen uniforms, but no Fae questioned their skill.

Rowan shut the door quietly.

The Royal Guards were well trained by Desdemona, whose philosophy was to master one weapon and demonstrate complete dominance with it. The House of Hathor guards, under Orion and Ora, trained with multiple bladed weapons, with the idea that the enemy would never know which one was your best; their short- and long-range weapons would suit any environment.

"Well?" Holly asked.

Rowan beckoned the others toward the center of the room. "Queen Sekhmet has put her House of Hathor guards at the door. Seems the Royal Guards didn't want to switch and were a bit confused by their new orders," he reported. "This is just my guess but, the bishops must have relieved Desdemona of her command of the Royal Guards, and it would seem the House of Hathor guards will be the new security in the palace. Queen Sekhmet isn't wasting time erasing the old regime."

Holly's nose twitched. "Perhaps I am wrong, but do you not find it odd your new queen did not ask her Oracle to be present for her coronation, Lady Sybella?" Holly inquired as the two Oracles stared out toward the windows.

"I would like to think Queen Sekhmet was trying to be respectful of the time I need to prepare for the eclipse," Lady Sybella said.

Rowan gave Holly a pointed look. He was not willing to give the new queen the benefit of the doubt.

Screams poured through the open balcony doors, and everyone ran to the balcony to see what was going on.

"Bloody hell!" The fox shook his head, his white fur sparkling in the sunlight. "These Fae make Nero appear rational, and this is all over what to do with Aurora's remains from what the guards were saying while we were roaming the halls. Why aren't the new guards dealing with this discord instead of guarding us?"

Lady Zarya had compassion in her eyes. "Yes, Aurora has become a polarizing figure even in death." She put her arm around the shoulders of the other Oracle, who wiped tears from her eyes.

"Still regal even in death," Lady Sybella whispered. Her former queen's remains held court in the center of the melee. "How does Aurora look tragically beautiful tied to a post? Her face is majestic, yet the sadness is not for her own passing. It's as if she knows the violence is unnecessary, like she is blaming herself when she is supposed to be resting." Sybella covered her face and cried.

Holly and Rowan could not help but be swept up in the image of the two Oracles comforting each other in this time of need. Even though they were from kingdoms with a contentious history, their shared grief unified them.

"The Oracles need us," Holly said, straightening. "We cannot allow this to affect them negatively. The eclipse is almost upon us. They must be focused."

"Aurora deserved better." Rowan's mood was somber.

Holly shook her head, unable to conceal the frustration in her soulful black eyes. She softened quickly. Rowan always had a big heart for his charges and wards. It was why the two Familiars worked so well together. Holly was logical, while he was passionate. "Rowan, we have been over this," she said. "I understand you liked Aurora, and so did I, but what's done is done. We must move forward. Bigger energies are at play. Get your head right, fox." The mink grabbed at his vest and climbed up the front of his body, using his clothing like a ladder. "Do you hear me? I need you. I need my partner in crime." She did not let him look away, cupping his cheeks between her paws. "You were my first protégé, do you remember? My first light. You were the first charge I ever gave my light, my essence to, and you know what is coming. How many stupid humans have we dealt with who thought the end was near? How many witches thought a fox's tail would bring them second sight? Or hunters wanted to turn me into a coat? We survived. Don't go and get all soft on me now!"

Rowan swallowed. "I love you too, Holly." He hugged her with one paw.

"That is not what I said." She playfully swatted him away as he set her down, but Rowan knew it was exactly what she was saying.

Rowan sniffed the air. The breeze brought a scent that he didn't recognize, and the smell led him in the direction of the bookcase. He crouched down, head low, ears pinned back, stalking closer as the scent became stronger. Rowan let out a low growl. He had found something— or someone.

"Rowan!" Lady Sybella's call had the pull of Magick in it. Rowan stopped his investigation, but he glanced back over his shoulder at the bookcase with narrowed eyes.

"Problem, my fox?" Lady Sybella asked.

"Not necessarily. I believe we may—"

He was interrupted by the sounds of fighting wafting up from the courtyard. Someone had thrown a barrel, and its metal hoop rolled across the platform. Aurora's body was still secured to the post, bloody from her passing. Rowan lost his train of thought.

"Where the hell are the bishops?" he asked, scanning the royal veranda.

"They slithered back under their rocks. That's what snakes do," Holly said.

Lady Zarya stroked Holly, who had climbed up around her neck for a better view. "I do not see King Jarvok or Lieutenant Zion."

"Perhaps they are on their way here," Holly said hopefully.

Lady Sybella let her fingers run down Rowan's back, more to soothe herself than him. She glanced skyward and closed her eyes. "It is almost time, Zarya. We have no choice but to proceed. I will share my prophecy stone if you will share yours." She met the other Oracle's silver eyes.

Lady Zarya gave Holly a quick look. "There has always been a representative of each court present for the prophecy readings. Our Familiars can act as the witnesses." She seemed relieved with the notion, but her Familiar gently dashed her plan.

"I am afraid we cannot, my lady. Rowan and I represent the Shadow Realm; it is our lineage. We cannot act as witnesses." She folded her small paws in a gesture of prayer as she spoke. The mink pressed on: "If there is no one to represent the courts, then Lady Sybella's solution to share each other's prophecy stone would be the best answer. I do sense some hesitation to the arrangement—may I inquire as to why?" Holly was trying to be gentle, and Rowan gave a nod of encouragement to his friend.

Lady Zarya shook her head. "There is no hesitation. I will share my stone if it is required and feasible, as long as

I accompany it. I do not feel comfortable leaving the stone. I am not accustomed to the new monarchy. That is all."

Lady Sybella jumped on board. "We will each accompany our stones to read the prophecies at our respective courts. The stones will stay in our care. I will accompany you to Blood Haven, and you will stay with me here in the Court of Light. Is that to your liking, Lady Zarya?"

The Dark Fae Oracle smiled. "Yes. Let us prepare." Despite her words, the energy wafting off Lady Zarya made the Familiars shiver.

"She knows something," Rowan whispered to Holly when the Oracles had returned indoors.

Holly's eyes narrowed. "I believe you are correct, my foxy friend."

"It seems she did not want to share the stone." Concern seeped into Rowan's voice.

"No, I don't believe it was about sharing the prophecy. This has to do with timing. She was fine with sharing the information during the eclipse as the prophecy happens; it is the part afterward that she is concerned with. She does not want to commit to having the stone," Holly said.

"Do you think she had a death vision? Or that she will be a target if she is in possession of the stone?" Rowan asked. He was worried that if Zarya was in danger—or if she died—his Oracle would not survive.

Holly shook her head. "I am unsure. I feel the eclipse is near. Come, Rowan, we can ponder what is happening with the Oracles' emotional state later; for now, let us be Familiars." She gracefully hopped down from the railing, her lithe body undulating across the floor. Rowan followed her inside, glancing once again in the direction of the bookcase as the strange scent wafted toward him. He wanted to check it out, but the moon's pull sent him to Lady Sybella's side. It was time.

"Rowan, once the eclipse starts, no one can enter this room. We must not be disturbed! If the monarchs are not here, too bad for them." Lady Sybella pointed at the door. "Your job is to protect us. This eclipse is a dark one, so Zarya will read first. Holly will act as a conduit to balance us both. You must see that no one interrupts us."

"May I use force?" the fox asked, his lips pulling away from his gums to reveal his long canines.

Sybella's eyes were cold. "Once we begin? Yes."

Chapter Four:
THE BUTTERFLY EFFECT

D esdemona fought to keep the mass of Fae from Aurora's body, but the crowd pushed closer, the platform swaying as they climbed up and pushed at the supports. Nightshade and Desdemona stood back-to-back and clashed with the few who dared to face them.

Chants of "Burn her!" and "Traitor!" echoed along with the screams and wails of the mourners.

Theadova and Malascola attempted to stop the fighting with reason, but their efforts were futile. "She would not want this" and "Let us honor her peacefully" did not stop the Fae from coming for the body. Some of the Heads of Houses pulled their factions away, though others lingered out of morbid curiosity. However, one Fae from a secondary house was not having any of it.

Lady Danaus waded into the crowd, thunder in her footsteps and grace in her aura. She had no fear. This Fae was on a mission. A trail of butterflies in an array of hues followed behind her, creating a comet's tail of red, orange, yellow, and blue in her wake. Her anger cut through the mass of Fae.

"Out of my way!" The fiery-coiffed Fae stomped to the middle of the fray, pushing Fae with one hand. With a wave of her right hand above her head, ten thousand monarch butterflies swooped down. "Enough!"

Lady Danaus pointed, and the butterflies formed a living wall between the fighting. When she spun her hands overhead, a sapphire glow poured from her fingertips. She directed a swarm of five thousand blue morpho butterflies to encircle Aurora's remains. Their cerulean and black wings blended together to protect the body.

The Fae watched, stunned into silence. No one had ever seen her command such power.

With an effortless jump, like she had wings of her own, Danaus ascended the platform. "Theadova and Malascola, Queen Sekhmet wants to speak with you. Word of your request has reached her, as well as the disrespectful behavior from the rest of you." She shot the crowd a disdainful glance, her lip curling. Her eyes softened around the edges when they met Malascola's. "Go now! I promise you no one will touch Aurora's remains until you return with our new queen's orders." She gazed back at the crowd, her eyes conveying a clear warning.

Theadova and Malascola bowed. "Thank you," Malascola mouthed.

Danaus watched them leave, making sure no one followed them. Her head whipped around like a snake's as she faced the lingering crowd. "If any of you are even thinking of testing me or these butterflies, go right ahead. I dare you! Because today, I am handing out smiles and lessons on decorum. Guess what? I am all out of smiles, my gentlefae.

Want to see why everyone thinks I am such a troll's wart?" There was a glint in her eye, and, in a flash, Lady Danaus brandished a broadsword over her head. The blade whistled through the air. "Any takers?"

Her butterflies tightened around Aurora's remains like a cocoon.

Many of the troublemakers dissipated after her outburst, but a stoic few folded their arms and refused to budge.

Danaus smirked. "Perfect. I needed the practice today." With a flick of her sword, she cut the train of her silk gown. "By the way, this," she held up the torn fabric, emblazoned with green butterflies," was my favorite gown." She threw it aside, and the silk sailed away on the breeze. She glanced up through her lashes and waved a finger. "Don't say I didn't warn you," she said, in a singsong. Despite the warning, the troublemakers rushed the platform.

Desdemona and Nightshade shared a look and a smile. "You know, I kind of like her," Nightshade said as they watched Danaus take on four rebel Fae without breaking a sweat. Lady Danaus used the hilt of her broadsword to hit one of them in the head and gave a front thrust kick to the stomach of the Fae to her left; without putting her leg down, she side-kicked another Fae, then stepped around him to introduce her elbow to his friend's forehead. A gash opened up on his brow, and he stumbled back as the blood poured down his face. Danaus hit him again with a crossing elbow to his jaw. He dropped and she stepped over his limp body. The four Fae lay in the dirt, clutching their respective injuries.

"Me too," Desdemona said.

Lady Danaus made her way over to them, her fight won. She bowed with her right hand over her heart.

"Thank you, Lady Danaus. You helped get the situation under control," Desdemona said as the rebels regrouped.

Lady Danaus waved her hand. "I respected Aurora a great deal. When Jayden met her Oblivion, Aurora visited and offered me comfort. It was a very difficult time, yet Aurora did her best to help me through losing my love. Even though she had lost one of her most formidable generals, and we were still at war with the Court of Dark, she always made time for me and my faction. I will not let her legacy be tarnished, much less her remains treated disrespectfully. I side with Theadova and Malascola; she should be buried in the Crystal Catacombs. I only hope our new queen agrees." Lady Danaus gazed up at the palace tower and let out a slow groan.

Lady Danaus was not a dreamer and did not let herself linger on what she felt was a wasted emotion. She had hoped too many times, to no avail. Her great love, Jayden, had met her Oblivion in the worst possible way, while battling an Acid-Breathing dragon at the Battle of Drystan.

Drystan had been an ambush, and Jayden had sacrificed herself to save her kin as Danaus knew only Jayden would. Danaus had wasted energy hoping that it was a mistake, and that Jayden would return to her. She wished the part of her heart that had melted along with Jayden would somehow become complete again with her miraculous homecoming, but only Jayden's quiver had returned, and in a pocket were Danaus' letters. Their love letters were reunited, but not the two of them. Danaus' heart was never made whole, and never would be again.

Lady Danaus shook her head to rid herself of the memories assaulting the partition of stoicism wrapped in the barbwire of indifference that protected her heart. Danaus had worked too hard to build the wall between her old life with Jayden and the Fae she was now.

Lady Danaus surveyed the remaining Fae dissidents and saw a chance to take her grief out on them. Her butterflies—sensing their guardian's pain—tightened together behind their mistress. The rebels would have to go through them to get to Danaus. Her butterflies not only kept her company, but they had Lady Danaus' best interests at heart. The butterflies funneled information to Danaus through their telepathic link. In her mind's eye, the butterflies showed her how many rebels there were and where they were gathering for their next attack.

"What do these morons hope to gain?" she asked. "I have a hard time believing any of them are invested in what happens to Aurora's remains. She faced resistance to her Unity with Jarvok, but I never heard the opposition was this extreme." Lady Danaus' eyes never wavered from the group, even as her butterflies sent her images of the horde from different angles. "Captain, my butterflies are telling me they are preparing for another go. We don't have much time. I can call for backup."

Desdemona ignored Danaus's warning, giving the mob a once-over. Something was nagging at her. *There is no common thread, all different factions, nothing linking them. The puzzle pieces don't fit.* "There is nothing in this for them. They seem to be fighting just to fight." *Is this really about Aurora wanting to unify the two lines?* A moment of clarity hit Desdemona as the thrumming of wings quieted her mind. "That's it! They aren't here to fight for the remains. They are a distraction!" Desdemona growled. "Tengu, Alvens—these are all—"

Nightshade turned in disbelief and confusion. "What? Why?"

Desdemona pointed up at the sun as the moon's shadow crept across it; the sunlight was already dimming. "Look, the eclipse has begun. And where are we?"

Lady Danaus glanced between the Illuminasqua.

"Damn it to Lucifer! The Oracles, the prophecy reading!" Nightshade yelled and threw her head back in frustration. "We cannot leave Aurora's remains unguarded."

"They were counting on that," Desdemona grumbled.

"Go. I can hold them." Lady Danaus gestured toward the palace.

Desdemona would not hear of it. "There are far too many."

"I told you I can call for backup," Lady Danaus said with a wicked twinkle in her eye. She raised her hands above her head, and a glowing yellow orb appeared. Lady Danaus extended her arms, palms touching over her head, and the globe grew brighter, orange tingeing the corona. She spun and brought her arms down around her body, mimicking wings. The yellow and orange energy trail grew from her palms to her forearms and wrapped around her waist. She dropped to her knees and let her fists hit the ground in a loud thunderclap.

The energy erupted through the ground, and another swarm of butterflies entered the courtyard, followed by a shriek from above. Desdemona looked up, expecting to see a dragon, but instead an enormous monarch butterfly the size of a dragon swooped down into the courtyard, causing many of the rebels to run for cover from the windstorm he whipped up. The butterfly landed on two Fae who were either too dumb or too stunned to move. They were crushed under his yellow and orange wings. "Illuminasqua, meet Sunshine, my backup." Lady Danaus winked at the butterfly, who bowed his head. Desdemona jumped to avoid the antennae. "Now would be a good time to exit, Illuminasqua," Lady Danaus urged.

"Umm... right. Guess I owe Indiga an apology. Little Big Mouth always seems to know things, like you, Lady Danaus, having a gigantic butterfly—and I told her not to believe everything she hears." Desdemona stared at the creature.

Nightshade leaned in. "So you told Indiga the gigantic butterfly didn't exist? Yeah, you owe her a big apology." The Illuminasqua gestured with her hands to emphasize the size of the butterfly that stood before them.

Desdemona rolled her eyes and smirked. "Little Big Mouth will never let me live this one down." A little levity seeped into the serious situation.

Lady Danaus stroked Sunshine like a dog, then turned to the remaining rebels. "I would run now. Sunshine is a carnivore, and I have not fed him today." As if taking his cue from her, Sunshine tore the leg off one of the crushed Fae; blue blood spurted upward from the artery, but the butterfly was unbothered by the mess, sucking the blood and detached tendons, through a straw-like extremity. The slurping sound did not seem to bother Danaus. Then he retracted it, and unlike any butterfly, Sunshine opened up a mouth full of razor-sharp teeth and took a bite from the torso before tossing the rest of the body up in the air and swallowing.

The bone crunching caught Nightshade's attention, and she looked over her shoulder to watch the butterfly eat the remains of the rebels. "You know I really, *really* like her. I may ask her to share some plum sugar wine after this," Nightshade said with a smirk, her cheeks rosy. Another roar from above caught their attention. "Okay, that was not a butterfly."

The two recognized Raycor, Zion's Acid-Breathing dragon, streaking across the sky. "Why is he leaving?" Nightshade asked. "Shouldn't Zion be in the reading?"

"He should, but so should the queen, and she requested to speak with Theadova and Malascola. They all should be in there already," Desdemona said.

Nightshade put her hand on Desdemona's shoulder. "I don't understand. Why isn't anyone in the reading?"

Desdemona sighed. She knew what she was about to say was going to change how Nightshade viewed the Court of Light, but it was gnawing at her, and Desdemona was positive her hunch was correct. "I think someone wants the Court of Dark kept out because they are afraid of what the Oracles will say. I think there are Fae who have secrets to keep. Some would kill for them, and others are willing to die to keep them."

Chapter Five:
THE WAITING GAME

S haking, Bishop Geddes pushed his way through the crowded room where the new queen sat. "I gave the orders to take her remains to the pyre, but the mob is uncontrollable," he said, breathless.

Jarvok and Asa exchanged a glance.

Sekhmet stood poised, composed and barely acknowledged the panic-stricken bishop.

Ora rushed in behind Geddes and quickly strode to her queen, whispering into her ear as she stared out the south-facing windows.

"Thank you, Ora. Keep me informed of what is happening," Sekhmet said as Ora bowed and left the room.

Bishops Caer and Bishop Ward went to Geddes to help calm him. Geddes panted as Caer got him some water. He didn't drink from the offered glass, falling instead into a chair.

The queen addressed the room. "Please, I ask that you remain here until the scuffle is quelled. I am going to speak with the leaders of this disagreement."

Bishop Geddes stood to protest, but Orion blocked him. "Your queen gave you a command, bishop," the guard said coldly. Bishop Geddes' jaw clenched, but he acquiesced.

Asa gave Jarvok a subtle tilt of her chin. He could practically hear her speaking in his head: *Be nice. We need to get to the reading.* "Of course, Queen Sekhmet," King Jarvok said. "We will wait here, but I must respectfully remind you: time is of the essence."

Ora returned and took her brother's place at the door as he prepared to escort the queen out.

Sekhmet glanced over her shoulder toward the Dark Fae king. "I am well aware, King Jarvok, of the time constraints. I will do my best to put this issue to rest in a timely fashion." She bowed her head and walked out, with Orion close behind her. Ora stayed put to act as security for the rest.

"Hell of a first day on the job for your queen," Jarvok remarked, but Ora merely rolled her eyes.

Jarvok turned to Asa and shrugged. "So much for being friendly," he said. "I tried."

"Maybe leave the charm to Zion, my liege." Asa patted him on the shoulder.

Jarvok gave a tight-lipped nod and went to the windows on the opposite side of the room, gesturing for his third-in-command to follow. Asa took the hint. "Did Zion return to Blood Haven with the High Council Guard?" Jarvok asked her in a hushed tone.

"Yes, my liege. As soon as it was done, he slipped out."

"Good. Once the Oracle reading is over, please see that Lady Zarya is escorted back to Blood Haven."

Asa remained impassive, careful to give nothing away to anyone watching them. "Yes, my liege." She had full confidence in Jarvok.

"If you two do not return by this evening's moonrise, I will have Drake, Construct, Ezekiel, Jennara, and Kali waiting to burn this palace to the ground. Do not take your time, Lieutenant."

"Understood, my liege. I will have Lady Zarya back at Blood Haven by moonrise." Asa rubbed at her temple. *Why did I answer like that?* But like a velvet voice guiding her, something in her gut told her to be careful with her wording. She shook off the feeling.

Jarvok eyed the bishops, who were huddled together. Caer glanced around and wrung his hands while Geddes swatted at him. Ward kept switching his staff from palm to palm.

"What do you make of that?" Jarvok asked, tipping his chin in the bishops' direction.

Asa closed her eyes and centered herself. When she opened them again, her white eye glowed. "Panic, anxiety. Geddes is desperate. They are hiding something. It is the motivation for their actions." As the glow from her eye dimmed, a dark-blue vein appeared on her neck and inched up toward her jaw. This would be where the new scar took root. Jarvok glanced at the deep-blue marking, and Zion's words from their heated discussion months ago came flooding back. Every time she used her gifts, she must make a sacrifice that marred her appearance. Jarvok realized she had added a new piece since the vernal equinox; her Kyanite armor now swooped down past the left side of her mouth toward her jaw. Before, it had stopped at the top of her lips.

Her hushed voice brought him back. "Shall I try to push past their walls to figure out what they are keeping hidden?"

The blue vein was like a viper writhing under her skin. "No, no. Thank you, Lieutenant Asa."

She narrowed her eyes and bowed.

A few steps away, the bishops loitered by the far window, next to the tapestry depicting the Shooting Star. Asa realized it was the same room where she and Zion had met Desdemona on the day of the banquet. *My, how times have changed.*

The bishops had their heads together; it was clear they were up to something, but it was no longer her concern. Jarvok had said not to poke around, and she knew better.

The room darkened, Asa glanced at her king, who nodded. They both knew what was happening—they could feel the pull of the moon, and the shadows were becoming sharper, more defined. Jarvok watched the floor as his helmet's shadow grew, the stalagmite points like fangs chewing on the quartz. In silhouette, Asa's own skull pauldrons looked as though they were screaming for mercy. The eclipse was very close.

The air became heavy with Magick; Jarvok knew the eclipse was riding his back like the wind off a mountain. It felt like a wave cresting. He understood he would not be present for the prophecy reading. But the sadness of the day was sinking into his bones. The eclipse was of no consequence to him. Lady Zarya would tell him of their reading, and if he needed to know more, he would have to deal with Sekhmet. *What could I possibly learn from today's eclipse?* He could not trust anything anymore–not even his own heart. He wanted to leave. Jarvok felt he had caused the disorder playing out in the courtyard, and he was certain the crowd blamed him for Aurora's death. In his mind, the Court of Light was founded on lies and broken trust; worst of all, he felt like a fool for thinking otherwise. The walls were closing in on him. He could almost hear the crowd chanting for his head. He wished they would storm the room. He was itching for a fight.

"My liege?" Asa put her hand on his shoulder. His Elestial Blade unsheathed itself as his paranoia bubbled to the surface. The Auric blade's light cast long shadows along the crystal walls. Ora took a defensive stance, reaching for her weapons belt. Jarvok looked at his blade, unaware why it had chosen that moment to show itself. This had happened once before, and Aurora had said it was due to emotions he had not dealt with. He counted backward from ten, trying to control his breathing.

Asa cautiously slid her hand to her king's forearm. She traced his scars, his skin hot under her cool touch. She closed her eyes and asked him to breathe with her. A pulse of energy snaked up his arm, ribbons in every color of the rainbow riding his veins to his heart. The blue color was extremely pale and thin, while the green was almost neon; the line was thick, like a boa constrictor.

Jarvok inhaled and exhaled with her, his breath settling.

"Your Chakras are spinning out of sync. My liege, allow me to help," Asa whispered.

Jarvok's fifth Chakra, the blue light—associated with the throat and speech—was dimming. *Many unexpressed emotions.* The green energy line of his heart Chakra was spinning too fast, denoting his grief. *Guilt, shame, sadness, what could have been—lost love.* Asa did her best to reset them, but she knew until he dealt with these feelings, they would continue to be a hindrance.

Jarvok's blade retracted, and he seemed calmer. "Thank you," the king mumbled. Everyone in the room stared at him, whether in shock or suspicion, he was unsure. Jarvok said nothing; he did not owe any of these Fae an explanation. To do so would be admitting guilt or weakness. He simply stalked over to Ora, who squared her shoulders, her chin tipped up. "Tell your queen I need to speak with her," Jarvok commanded.

Chapter Six:
DIPLOMACY

Theadova and Malascola entered what was formerly known as Aurora's library, only now it was unrecognizable. The crystal-blue sodalite shelves Malascola had built for Aurora to store her beloved books were gone, ripped out of the walls. The polished dark-blue crystal with its white veins had been masterfully set into the walls, with thirty shelves from floor to ceiling. The fluted columns on the ends once held bright-yellow raw clusters of citrine to contrast the hues of blue. They had looked like crowns sitting atop the columns, proud and majestic.

Malascola remembered scouring the deepest caverns to find the perfect shade of citrine to complement the blue of the sodalite. Aurora's voice echoed in his head: "Yes, Malascola, sodalite for the library. We are all prone to overthinking and getting caught up in the future instead of what is important in the present. Sodalite helps to calm and center us. It is the perfect stone for reading and studying." He had argued back and forth with the queen, telling her to use amethyst to aid in concentration, but

Aurora had been correct. Fae from all over the Veil came to study in Aurora's private library. Now, as he examined the room, he saw it was no longer the library he had worked on tirelessly for the queen he adored. Instead of the book-cases, there were gilded floor-to-ceiling frames, most likely to hold portraits of Queen Sekhmet. The fluorite floors that Malascola had so delicately laid by hand was marred by a large gold sequoia tree symbolizing the new queen's faction: the House of Hathor.

"When did she have time for this? She was only crowned a few hours ago," he mumbled as he stroked and pulled his mustache.

Theadova rested his cheek on the pink silk pillows adorning the new chairs and then stomped his cloven hooves on the rugs. "Where are Aurora's books?" There were tears in the deer's dark-purple eyes. In the dim light of the library, they appeared nearly black. "Aurora adored her books. This library was partly an homage to Serena. If you listen, you can hear the waves crashing on the rocks. Isn't that why this room is an octagon, to help the sound bounce off the walls?"

Malascola nodded. "Aurora wanted to hear the waves crashing, but it's not quite an octagon." He gestured for the stag to look up. "The ceiling spirals like the inside of a conch shell."

"Malascola, I want to run out. There were too many memories," Theadova said.

"I know. Me too." Malascola hunched his shoulders.

What Sekhmet had done to Aurora's sanctuary was blasphemous. But they had one final favor to do for their queen and dear friend.

Theadova nodded toward the corner. "Look, Malascola."

Alone in the corner stood Aurora's writing desk, the only part left of her in that room. The dark wood of the legs was engraved with septagrams, crystals inlaid amongst the seven-pointed stars. Malascola smiled, remembering how he and Hogal had constructed the desk for her. The chair was a miniature version of her throne. "Hogal's idea," the Gnome said, pointing to it. The two Fae chuckled. Hogal wanted all the chairs in the palace that belonged to Aurora to look like her throne. He would insist that "a queens be only sitting on a throne."

"She always loved reading and writing in the corner where the sunlight hit in the late afternoon," Malascola said with a soft smile. The smile faded as he noticed the desk was covered with maps and parchments, none of which belonged to Aurora.

Before the two could explore the contents of the desk, Orion and Queen Sekhmet entered the room.

Startled, Theadova almost knocked over the desk chair. The Gnome and stag bumped into each other like young dragons learning to walk. Finally, they composed themselves, Malascola crossing his ankles as he leaned against Theadova's side, whistling. Both were so embarrassed at their bumbling they had nearly forgotten why they were there.

Orion's eyebrows arched, but he ignored their inelegance. "I present Queen Sekhmet. Kneel before your queen."

Theadova and Malascola exchanged a glance but complied. They needed Sekhmet to grant Aurora's last wish, and being stubborn would not help their cause.

"Please rise," Sekhmet said.

She made herself comfortable on one of her pink chairs. Orion stood rigid behind her.

"Malascola, you must be taken aback by the changes in this room." Sekhmet opened her hands in a wide gesture.

Malascola licked his lips. *Careful, I must be careful with my answer.*

"It suits you, Your Grace," Theadova blurted out, obviously uncomfortable with the silence.

Sekhmet stared at her nails. "I did not ask you, white stag." She flipped her wrist at the Spelaion. "I asked him."

Malascola raised his chin as if gathering his fortitude. "It is fitting for a queen as lovely as yourself." He gave a dramatic bow.

Theadova exhaled in relief.

Sekhmet smiled. "I know your faction completed most of the work in the room for Aurora. You must have been surprised to see such changes, but some of my followers insisted on giving me this as a gift." She glanced around the room, her fingers grazing the fuchsia pillow. "It was done in more of my taste. They work fast." Her blue eyes flashed jade, as if she were testing the Fae.

Malascola took the bait. "What happened to the books? Ah, Your Grace." He bowed quickly.

"The books? Oh, those dusty remnants. I had them put in storage or whatever." She waved vaguely. It was clear Sekhmet had no idea where Aurora's books had gone, nor did she care.

The top of Malascola's head turned red with anger. Orion took a slight step forward.

Theadova interceded. "Your Grace, we have a parchment stating that Aurora's last wish was to be buried in the Crystal Catacombs. We humbly ask you to honor her request." The leader of the Aubane Faction lowered his neck, the blossoms on his gilded antlers grazing the floor.

Sekhmet's eyes flicked to Malascola, who went to bended knee. The queen relaxed into her chair and rubbed her palms along the velvet armrests. "May I see the parchment?"

Malascola produced a wrapped scroll complete with Aurora's unbroken seal.

Sekhmet cracked the wax, and the room was filled with the scent of lilac, vanilla, and sunshine. Theadova inhaled, his black nostrils flaring. "Aurora," he whispered.

Thunder boomed in the distance. Sekhmet unrolled the cylinder and scanned the writing.

Theadova and Malascola stayed in a position of humility, afraid that any sudden movement might change the new queen's mood or mind.

"Your wish is granted," Sekhmet said softly.

"Huh?" Malascola jerked his head up.

"Your Grace, thank you," Theadova said. "You are a wonderful successor; I am humbled by your wisdom."

Sekhmet stood and glided across the floor. Her fingers brushed against the white stag's cheek, causing him to look up. "Aurora's wishes should be honored. I will write a decree. Hathor guards will escort you both to the courtyard to make my command known." She leaned in, whispering into his ear. "After this is settled, you and I will finish that conversation, Theadova. The one about you becoming a parent. We started it so long ago at the banquet." She winked at him. Theadova's mouth hung open.

Sekhmet returned to her seat and ordered Orion to assign Hathor guards to see that Aurora's remains were placed in the Crystal Catacombs. The queen smirked. "Oh, and Malascola? Remember at the banquet when you told me to move along, that I wasn't your queen?"

Malascola grimaced at the memory. "Yes, Your Grace, I do recall I may have said something to that effect, which at the—"

Sekhmet held her hand up. "My, how times have changed. You are dismissed."

Theadova and Malascola made eye contact with each other, relieved, but deep down they also knew a price would be paid for this charitable gesture by the new queen. They wondered which of the two would pay. Theadova swallowed; he had a sneaking suspicion it would be him. But judging by how pale Malascola was, it was clear the new queen could be a petty Fae. A petty Fae with power was nothing to write off.

Chapter Seven:
Moving Forward

J arvok stared Ora down. The House of Hathor guard had her hand on her sickle. For a moment, her eyes flicked to Asa who stood just behind her king, ready to do whatever he needed her to. Ora's gaze returned to the Dark Fae King.

"I need to see Sekhmet." Jarvok's voice was quiet but authoritative. "The prophecy is starting. I am not a prisoner, Ora."

"No! You displayed your weapon. I will not allow you near my queen," Ora said.

Before Jarvok could make a move, Sekhmet strode in. "He most definitely can speak with me, Ora. Stand down," the queen said.

Ora opened her mouth to protest, but the look on Orion's face told her not to. She stepped to the side and allowed Jarvok to pass. Asa's gaze lingered on the Vila twins. Ora and Orion stared back at her, and unspoken challenge flowed between them all. Finally, Ora glanced down, and the Dark Fae held Orion's gaze. Something told her they were destined to dance one day.

"Lieutenant Asa, I would like to speak with King Jarvok alone. Monarch to monarch, as long as your king does not object," Sekhmet said in a melodic voice.

Jarvok gave a subtle tilt of his chin. "Yes, Your Grace." *And this is why I asked Asa to stay and not Zion; there is no way he would have agreed or even acted courteously. Nor could I leave Zion alone with the twins without returning to a fight.*

He followed Sekhmet down the hallway to a lavishly decorated sitting room. His first impression was that the room was not done in Aurora's taste; he did not know this was once Aurora's library. She had not been so ostentatious. Either Queen Sekhmet moved very quickly, or there was more about his former lover he did not know. Both possibilities made him uneasy.

Sekhmet had two gold goblets of plum sugar wine at the ready, though Jarvok politely declined. Sekhmet took a delicate sip before she offered him a seat. The Dark Fae King remained standing as she settled into a gilded chair with pink upholstery.

Sekhmet glanced up at him through her long pastel lashes. "I spoke with Malascola and Theadova. I gave them permission to lay Aurora's remains to rest in the Crystal Catacombs per her last wishes. I sincerely hope this will not be a point of contention between us."

Jarvok pursed his lips. "Her remains are not my concern, but I find your decision most magnanimous as a new queen. Your Grace, I appreciate you wanting to share this with me. However, it is clear the eclipse is upon us, and we cannot disturb the Oracles." He was hoping to get a feel for Sekhmet's priorities.

"I agree," she said. "We cannot disturb them. This is why I wanted to discuss a deal with you. I will share the Light Oracle's reading with you—" She pointed gracefully at him. "—if you in turn will share the Dark Oracle's reading with me."

Jarvok ran his hand along the back of the empty chair as he pondered her request. "I can share, but not today. We will arrange a meeting at the Archway of Apala in the coming days, contingent upon my Oracle leaving after the reading without any incident. Lady Zarya and Lieutenant Asa are to be granted safe passage from the Court of Light. Should anything happen to them, the deal is off. Are we clear?"

And, if you refuse, members of my Blaze Battalion will come charging in, but you don't need to know that. Diplomacy, Jarvok, good for you! See, I can be taught.

Sekhmet nodded. "Of course, King Jarvok. They will have no issues with my Fae."

"Then I have no qualms about sharing my reading with you."

Sekhmet smiled and stood to pour herself another goblet of wine. "Wonderful. And I have something else I would like to discuss with you."

"And that is?"

"How we are to move forward as monarchs ... together."

Jarvok raised an eyebrow. *If you think I am getting involved with another queen, you, my dear, are out of your Faeking mind.*

She placed her goblet down and glided past him to an ornate desk covered with scrolls and parchments. Sekhmet unrolled a scroll with care and placed crystals at the corners to hold it flat.

Jarvok stared at the parchment, the blue-black ink coming into focus. He rubbed his chin as he scanned the map, labeled with cartographical symbols. "What is this?" he asked, but Sekhmet only set a primitive sculpture on the table next to the parchment.

From Jarvok's perspective, the sculpture looked like the top half of an egg, though more pointed. It was decorated with flowers. Two similar objects were set beside it, each demonstrating artistic sophistication. The last one was smooth and made of bluestone. He recognized the rock from the stone cult circles in southern England because it hummed with power, that energy signature marked the difference between the types of stones.

This egg had a serpent design winding around it and a small hole drilled into the side. "Grecian," he observed.

"Yes. Delos omphalos. From our temple in Greece—the Delphi site, to be exact. Translated, *omphalos* means navel."

Jarvok recalled the small island revered by the Greeks and their surrounding neighbors. It was the site of the human oracles who acted as emissaries to the Fae during their time as Greek gods. He recalled seeing larger, less ornate sculptures at temples around the area too. "I believe we told the humans it was part of the Titan myth. We have been gods to so many religions, I cannot keep our mythos straight anymore." He waved a hand.

"Close enough, King Jarvok. The navel stone has been found at many of our temples, from Greece to Egypt. It represents the humans' connection to the earth, but for us, it is so much more." She held up the bluestone, examining it.

"I am listening," Jarvok replied, not sure why this was relevant. *I am getting annoyed, Sekhmet. I don't need a lesson on my own history.*

She glanced up at him and smiled. "Aurora was very well versed in elemental Magick. The sites she directed the humans to build temples and shrines on were by design, Jarvok."

He conceded that. The Dark Fae did not have the same connection to the elements that the Light Fae did, and he had followed the lead of the Court of Light when it came to temple sites. He simply instructed his worshippers to build his shrines alongside those erected by his Light Fae counterparts.

Sekhmet cleared her throat and pointed to the map with markings. "The suns represent our temples. The moons represent yours. It may be esoteric, but it works." She unrolled another scroll over the map. This one had the same markings, but with red conical symbols. "The red indicates where we have found navel stones."

Jarvok examined the sites. He was not aware the navel stones were found in all these areas; they were not part of all the myths of creation.

"The humans used the stones to symbolize life and earth, the physical representation of the umbilical connection to the earth. What they did not know is that the stones could harness the energies of the earth when made from the right type of material." She unrolled the last scroll, this one with the same markings overlaid with symbols representing the body's Chakras. "Notice the pattern with the earth navels, the earth Chakras, and our temples."

Jarvok ran his finger over the scroll, following the lines from the root Chakra in the far west to the sacral Chakra south of it, then across the map and looping around the land masses to the crown Chakra in the easterly mountains. He noticed the Chakras with higher vibrations—the throat, solar plexus, and the third eye—had elevated concentrations of earth navels. "Earth Chakras?" Jarvok hated to ask the obvious question, but he had no choice.

Queen Sekhmet arched an eyebrow at him. "Aurora never explained the earth Chakras to you? I would have thought in your time together... It is of no consequence; I will not withhold such information." She shrugged. Jarvok stayed impassive, letting her take her jabs. *Go ahead, Sekhmet. Have your fun. I will not bite—not now—but watch your tone, new queen, or I will clip those leaves. They are still rebuilding the tower from when Aurora and I tussled, and something tells me you aren't nearly as much fun as she was.* Jarvok slid his hand over his mouth to cover his smirk at the memory of his fight with Aurora. Luckily, Sekhmet did not notice, too caught up in her explanation.

"Just as the Fae and even the humans have energy centers, our Earth has her own," she said. "Just as our Chakras allow us to tap into our energetic and elemental gifts, the Earth's Chakras draw on her energy system. And like us, when they are out of balance, things do not function the same."

Sekhmet pointed out the seven Chakra sites, where the energy of the associated element was strongest because of its purity. The site of the Great Pyramid of Egypt was marked by an indigo circle with an upside-down triangle in the middle. "That is the throat Chakra," the queen said. "If you remember this area before the plagues and the enslavement of the Israelites, they were known for their ability to express themselves. They invented papyrus. Even gender in the beginning was less of an issue than in many of our modern cultures. Freedom of speech was valued too. However, since the unrest, I have watched the breakdown of communication and self-expression. We have not seen a more creative culture come forth since. As the throat Chakra becomes more unbalanced, the region will continue to see turmoil."

Jarvok stroked his chin, thinking over the queen's words. "You are eloquent in your explanation, Sekhmet. It seems obvious these vortices are present." He gestured at the scrolls, urging her on.

"The throat Chakra is also the birthplace of the major religious movements; the prophets have all made a move here. Moses, Mohammed, and Jesus all preached in this general vicinity, delivering the word of their respective religions in the fifth Chakra's influence. However, this is only one example of how the earth Chakras manifest." She pointed west. "Here is an active volcano at the root Chakra, which erupts with the energy from deep within the earth." She looked at Jarvok, who once again nodded at her to continue. "From each Chakra, lines of energy flow like veins from our heart, delivering energy to the earth. There are also lines that feed electromagnetic energy to the Chakras like the neurons in our brains. These lines give Mother Earth information about her world. Where these two types of lines intersect are very powerful spots, and this is where Aurora had her temples built. She did this to help charge the earth—and us."

Jarvok considered how easily his Fae were able to tap into their own energy and generate plasma to defend themselves in these particular locations. He had always chalked it up to the power of worship. He frowned now, understanding it had been something so much more. He had been naive. The Dark Fae king took a deep breath and tried to regain his stoic expression, not wanting his lack of understanding to define their relationship. "Your Grace, while I appreciate the education, how does this affect us moving forward?" *Just get on with it, Fae.*

Sekhmet curled her lips. "Ah, and there it is, the Dark Fae's cut-to-the-chase attitude. The Light Fae do have a tendency to overexplain, or in some cases do not explain anything. Don't you agree?"

Jarvok stared at her. *And?*

Sekhmet shrugged. "My apologies. As you experienced, bluestone can store energy. I want to harness the energy at these intersecting lines—I call them Fae lines—with the bluestone. I believe they will act as magnets and slingshots to help us travel the Veil more efficiently." She raised her chin, obviously proud of her revelation.

"The Court of Dark travels just fine through the Veil," Jarvok said curtly. *Like I would tell you anything.*

Sekhmet put her hands up in surrender. "We are all aware of your mysterious ways of traveling across the Veil and your desire for it to stay that way. I am not asking you to divulge your secrets. My point is that these stones will allow us to zero in on the energy pulsations, much as you did when you held it. Thus, I believe we can use them to pull ourselves to a certain point in the Veil without expending extra energy."

"So, what you are saying is that the bluestones could provide us with more landing options when we travel through the Veil? Is that the only advantage?" Jarvok asked, eyeing the queen.

"Yes, King Jarvok. We wouldn't have to arrive at elemental crossroads or wait to be summoned by our cults to hone in on that specific power surge. But if you are asking me if the stones have other applications, they do not." Her expression seemed vague, detached.

"And why should I believe you?" Jarvok said, holding the Grecian earth navel. *Do not answer because it wouldn't matter, I will never believe you.*

"You do not have to, but I have been most forthcoming when I did not have to share anything with you. Nor have I inquired as to why no Light Fae can see Blood Haven from the top of the Niamia Falls or the Smoking Mountain." She raised an eyebrow at him.

Jarvok didn't flinch. *I am not a baby dragon looking for my mother to show me how to fly.* "Oh, but you did need to share this information. You need my help in placing more earth navels around our temples, or else it would be a violation of the treaty."

Sekhmet smirked but bowed her head.

Jarvok tossed the earth navel from hand to hand, gauging her expression. "I will need a demonstration of your hypothesis before I commit. I would assume the stone circle cult would be the most appropriate site?" *With the Dark Fae way of traversing the Veil, we travel very accurately, but this would ingratiate her to me and show I can cooperate. Furthermore, this proves she has no idea how we travel, so I shall concede to this for now. But I may draw it out.*

"You have an acute mind for this project, King Jarvok. I am happy to demonstrate the potential this holds for both courts."

Jarvok motioned toward the door. "Send a messenger when you have the testing set up. Now, if you do not mind, I have more than fulfilled my obligations for today. Lieutenant Asa will be in charge of escorting Lady Zarya back to Blood Haven, and I will take my leave." Jarvok tipped his head and turned to exit, but Queen Sekhmet called him back. He blew out a breath and rolled his eyes before he turned to face her. "Yes?" *Now what?*

Sekhmet stood and smoothed out her gown, letting her hands linger at her waist for a moment as she met his eyes. "Thank you for your time. I look forward to a mutually beneficial relationship with the Court of Dark." Jarvok curtly nodded and exited the queen's private chambers. *Nice try, Sekhmet. I'll give you points for your attempt.*

Queen Sekhmet twirled in front of her chair and settled back into it, rubbing the armrests in a sensual way. This was going so much better than she had hoped. She drank the rest of the wine and licked her lips, relishing the sweetness. "Much better," she whispered to the empty room.

When Jarvok returned to the room where the others waited, Asa rose and walked briskly to meet him. "My liege, is everything satisfactory?"

Jarvok scanned the room. He knew the bishops were eavesdropping; they must choose their words carefully. "Yes, and I trust you will carry out my orders regarding Lady Zarya. I have been assured by Queen Sekhmet you are both to be granted safe passage from the palace."

Asa frowned. "Are you leaving?"

"I have one last detail to take care of. I will see you at Blood Haven with Lady Zarya." Jarvok did not wait for

Asa to respond. He had faith in her to follow through with his orders.

The bishops were still plotting. Geddes seemed physically calmer, but the group had moved to the corner, making a wall with their bodies as they stood shoulder to shoulder. Ward glanced up, more to see who was looking at them than anything else.

Jarvok prepared to leave, but Ora and Orion blocked the door. The two guards seemed steadfast in their resolve. Nothing was getting past them.

"I suggest you move," Jarvok growled, but Orion snarled back. Asa sidled up behind her king. Jarvok's eyes bored through the House of Hathor guards. "I will not repeat myself," the king said coldly. "I am no longer under protective custody. I have been given permission by your queen to depart."

Jarvok took a step closer to Orion.

"Orion! King Jarvok has permission to leave of his own accord, and I need to speak with you," Sekhmet called from the hall. As if broken from a trance, Orion blinked.

Jarvok patted the guard on the shoulder and pushed him aside. Orion watched the Dark Fae King exit and then bowed to his queen. Despite the bishops' protests, he left them in the care of his surly sister.

Orion walked into Sekhmet's private quarters. "Keep the bishops in there until the eclipse is over, the lieutenant is allowed to leave with the Dark Oracle. Jarvok has agreed to my terms and will share the reading with us," the queen ordered, without preamble.

"And the bluestones?" Orion asked.

"He wants a test of their capabilities at the stone circle cult. He suspects they might be more useful, but we can throw him off. Are you sure you destroyed all the information regarding Atlantis, Orion? You planted the false tablets?" Sekhmet searched the eyes of her most trusted guard.

"Yes, my queen."

"Very good."

Jarvok was not stupid, and Sekhmet did not want him to realize the stones' true nature—not until she got what she wanted out of him. By then it would be far too late for the Dark Fae.

She dismissed Orion and picked up an oversized gold box. Sekhmet bit her bottom lip as she gazed lovingly at its contents. *Now it is time for me to shed the mundane trappings these simple plebeians call regal trinkets and show them what it truly means to be the Queen of the Court of Light.*

Chapter Eight:
A Promise Fulfilled

Malascola and Theadova walked toward the courtyard accompanied by two House of Hathor guards. Their metallic uniforms were eye-catching, especially in contrast with the crystalline hallways. Reflections of gold bounced off the walls with each step.

Outside the castle, pandemonium reigned. Disembodied limbs of dissident Fae were strewn around the platform's supports. On the platform, a cocoon of blue butterflies shielded Aurora's remains with their beating wings. But the most unexpected sight was the twenty-foot butterfly eating dead Fae while Lady Danaus fought off any other Fae dumb enough to approach the platform.

"What, by all that is light in the universe, is going on?" Malascola cried out.

Danaus swung her head toward the group as she dropped to one knee and swung her broadsword in a wide arc, taking out a rebel Fae. "More for you, Sunshine."

The butterfly responded by crunching the arm of the fallen Fae.

Danaus brushed her sweaty hair off her brow. "Malascola, Theadova! Nice of you to join me. Do you come with good news?"

The Hathor guards stared up at the butterfly.

"Hey, you were sent here by the queen," Malascola urged. "Get up there and make the announcement. Help the lady out."

The guards shook their heads.

Malascola rolled his eyes. "Danaus, luv, can you call off Sunshine? Seems these two are a bit afraid of your butterfly."

Danaus smirked as she kicked another rebel. "I am kind of busy here, Mally, but sure, anything for the big, strong Hathor guards." She stroked the carnivorous butterfly until his back leg thumped. "Who's a good boy? Now go stand next to Aurora's body for me."

Sunshine backed up, moving with grace and precision.

Using her broadsword, Danaus waved the guards onto the platform along with Theadova and Malascola.

Malascola slapped one of the guards on the leg to hurry him along. "Well? Get on with it! These rebels aren't going to stand here all day! The eclipse is upon us."

The guard walked to the front of the platform, looking over his shoulder as he produced a scroll. He cracked the wax seal bearing the new queen's insignia—a sequoia tree with a crown over the branches—and carefully unrolled the parchment. "By royal decree of Her Highness Queen Sekhmet! Aurora, last and only Sylph, will be laid to rest in the Crystal Catacombs. Any Fae who stands against this decree will be seen as acting in the way of treason, a crime punishable by Oblivion. Queen Sekhmet says for all to go home; the fighting ends now. Her word is law."

Many Fae threw down their makeshift weapons and abandoned their cause. Some stayed to hurl insults, but the fighting ceased. Malascola and Theadova both slumped in relief. Lady Danaus glanced up toward the Contemplation Room, knowing the prophecy reading was set to begin.

"Lady Danaus, if you could ask your butterflies to release Aurora, we will prepare the body," Theadova said gently.

The Fae gave a thin-lipped smile. Her job was finished. "Yes, of course." She positioned her palms at her heart, and with a quick push outward, she separated her hands. Light-blue energy pulsed. When the light dissipated like sugar dissolving in the rain, the butterflies fluttered away from Aurora's body.

Aurora's head was still upright. Desdemona had secured Aurora's ankles, knees, hips, waist, shoulders, and forehead to the black crystal pole to keep the body as straight as possible, but her body was showing signs of stress. Her shins were beginning to twist at an odd angle and her neck leaned to the left in an unnatural curve. Her beautiful turquoise eyes were closed, but tear tracks still stained her cheeks. Her complexion was starting to turn to a grey pasty pallor and her lips were stained with blood. Her hands were discolored from the blood pooling in them, shades of blue and purple mottled her fingers.

Theadova gasped and turned away. "I do not want to remember her like this."

Malascola swallowed, his throat bobbing as if he was swallowing his emotions, trying to stay strong for Aurora. He rested his calloused hand on his friend's back for a moment in an attempt at comfort. "I'll get her."

The Gnome walked up to Aurora's body, Lady Danaus following, but he put his palm up to stop her. She folded her hands together, respectful of his wishes. Malascola turned his forearm to expose the underside of his shimmering gauntlets. There was a small hole about three finger breadths from his wrist. He stood back, outstretched his arm, took aim, and closing his fist, aimed at the ropes holding Aurora's head, clear liquid shot from the hole and ate through the ropes. Aurora's chin dropped to her chest, and Malascola went to the back of the pole and took care of the ropes behind her. He moved systemically around her body, disintegrating her bindings with his acid until she slumped forward. He was there to catch the fallen queen, cradling her in his arms. Silently he wept, holding his friend in his arms gently like she was sleeping, and he was afraid of waking her with his hysterics.

Theadova and Danaus waited until the sobbing Gnome fell to the platform with the body of Queen Aurora in his arms. Malascola's tears mixed with the dried blood, and rivulets of blue traveled down the bodice of her dress, catching on the small rows of embroidered flowers at her waist. His tears resembled raindrops from a summer's rainstorm clinging to the petals.

"We need to find Hogal," Theadova whispered to Danaus.

"I will bring him to you when you are ready. But for now, let us take care of Malascola," Lady Danaus replied. She knew the signs of heartbreak, of someone who had held it all in for far too long.

Theadova and Danaus crouched down, their arms encircling Malascola. Danaus's smaller butterflies flew in a frenetic pattern above, a cloud of colors sensing their guardian's pain.

"Will you come with us to the catacombs?" Theadova met her eyes as the tears fell.

She shook her head. "No. I loved our queen, but you, Malascola, and Hogal had a different bond with her. Let me be the one to assist in prepping her for burial." Her voice hitched.

Sunshine kept watch over the three Fae, his antennae twitching and wings steady. The universe would have to grant mercy to any Fae who dared to disturb them, for they would face his wrath.

Chapter Nine:
RELIGULOUS

R owan sat at attention facing the arched rose quartz double doors, their intricate carvings and stained glass no longer casting rainbow reflections on the floor. Should anyone or anything try to disturb Holly or the Oracles during the prophecy reading, they would need to go through him. The impending eclipse crept across his fur, raising his hackles. The boundaries between worlds, including the Shadow Realm, were thinnest during a solar eclipse. It was the time when all of the worlds were drenched in the darkness of Mother Luna's power—her reach felt by all. It was her special gift; a reminder that nothing escaped her sight, that at times light would be overtaken by darkness. As a creature of the Shadow Realm, he was acquainted with the darkness, but he preferred to walk in the light. Nay, he *relished* dancing in the light. Perhaps that was why he tried to be empathetic toward his wards.

Rowan had seen the horrible side of humanity, especially with monarchs. They epitomized selfishness, indulging their egos. They cheated on their spouses, who they married for political necessity. They taxed their subjects mercilessly; their people starved while they ate like pigs going to the slaughter. They felt they were entitled to loyalty yet gave no respect. They chased money and power over finding their own moral compass.

When he met Aurora and Jarvok, he had felt a glimmer of hope. Together, he thought, their combined strengths and weaknesses could lead to a strong kingdom that would unify the Fae and help the humans who seemed to be heading down the wrong path. This was his wish until one of his "cousins," for lack of a better term, the Shadow Kat was set loose upon Aurora. Wearing the skin of her former Bishop Awynn, the Shadow Kat had preyed upon her insecurities as a ruler and in her relationship with Jarvok. With the Oracles' help, Rowan and Holly had revealed the Shadow Kat to Aurora in her dream, but who sent the creature after her no one knew. The damage was done, and now Rowan stood guard after a very good ruler's execution. She had been the first in a long time who had renewed his faith in a monarch. Now Mother Luna was about to douse the world in her darkness and give the Oracles a prophecy of doom and gloom, because that was what she did at times like this. Whenever things looked bad, she would either shower you with flowers or remind you things could get much worse. And he had already received a shower of flowers the other day. "Oh, bloody hell," Rowan whispered.

He wasn't the only one feeling this way. Both Oracles seemed on edge—picking up objects and putting them down, only to repeat the process moments later. Zarya constantly fixed her hair, while Sybella kept looking for her cloak even though it was right in front of her. Though they were not privy to Mother Luna's existence, they still sensed the nervous energy shift that came with her presence.

On the surface, the Fae touted a structure of universal energies that guided them, a synergistic system blending the four elements of nature with the sun, moon, and the Magick of spirit residing in all living creatures. This created the energy and powers that made the universe work. *Deep down, the older Fae who were originally Virtue Angels believe their Creator is the be-all-end-all. Silly ol' Fae! That primitive thinking is for lower life forms*, Rowan mused, shaking his head. *If they only knew how many realms there are and that their "God" is merely one incarnation of the universal energies. Hell, humans are even further behind the Fae.* And at the rate they were regressing, he had almost no faith they would ever catch up.

As Christianity gained popularity, he had witnessed the religion being used by rulers for their own personal vendettas, prejudices, and desires. They fought among themselves while waging a war against other faiths, which had their own sects. However, all agreed that paganism was the real enemy, so those closest to the true pattern of universe were generally reviled. That had been part of the reason Aurora planned to join the two courts: to protect paganism. Rowan could only hope the new queen would follow Aurora's plan to strengthen the foundation of paganism before humanity turned its back on the Fae.

Rowan's noticed the wavy pattern of light on the floor, like the reflection of water on the crystal walkway. The chill in the air grew with the sense of unease, but there was energy to it. The atmosphere in the room crackled and popped; as he inhaled, it felt thick in his lungs. It took effort to lift his head and gaze out toward the balcony at the three figures standing in the doorway. All the doors were open in the room, the air filled with a pungent, yet fresh, aroma. The atmosphere was charged, the scent just before and after lightning strikes its target, ozone, rain, heat, and destruction like a fire had scorched the earth. *It has begun.*

Chapter Ten:
THE PROPHECY

L ady Zarya bowed her head, her hood pulled up to cover her face. The silver fabric of her cloak still seemed to glisten despite the lack of light, like the full moon in the summer night when it owns the sky. Small crescent moons were embroidered down the front of her silken cloak, their edges interlocked like shaking hands. A pyrite crescent moon closure secured the garment at her throat; the stone looked cool against her skin. Lady Sybella stood on her right, dressed in a gold cloak with a sunstone closure and suns embroidered on the silk in a matching design to Zarya's moons. Holly stood between them in nothing but her fur. The mink looked down at herself a few times, feeling a bit under dressed compared to the Fae.

Well, the Oracles do know how to dress for an occasion.

Holly watched as the Oracles gave her a soft smile and their shoulders relaxed at her presence, clearly, she was a comfort to both Oracles.

The Dark Oracle raised her head and signaled for them to drop to their knees. The group knelt with their foreheads on the floor for a breath until Zarya sat up. Zarya removed her hood and folded her hands in her lap, then Sybella did the same. In unison, they walked to the altar table set up inside the room.

The table was narrow, with carvings on the apron featuring the sun and the phases of the moon. Each celestial body was depicted with a crystal: amber for the sun and moonstone for the moon. Constellations were set behind the phases of the moon with clear quartz. A large gold candlestick holder stood at each end of the table, holding a white candle awaiting a flame. The group moved slower now, like walking in molasses; even the smallest movements took effort for the Oracles. Fatigue flashed across Sybella's face as she reached the altar and steadied herself. The Magick was thick in the air now that the eclipse was upon them. Before, it was like a heavy blanket, warm and comforting. Now, it was squeezing them, begging for them to release the pent-up power and unleash it through the prophecy.

The room grew dimmer in the moment it took for the Oracles to check that they had the materials needed for the prophecy readings. Two pieces of parchment sat at each side for them, along with their blank prophecy stones: a sunstone disc for the Oracle of Light and a moonstone disc for the Oracle of Dark. As they received their message, the prophecy would travel through the Oracles and magically inscribe itself onto the stones in a language only decipherable by a Fae of that lineage. A bowl of white sage burned in the center to cleanse the energy in the air, the sweet cedar-laced aroma floating through the room.

Holly was trying to maneuver a piece of chalk almost as big as her arm. She had finished drawing a sun on the floor where Sybella would stand and was putting the final touches on the crescent moon for Zarya. When Holly finished the image, she hopped on top of the altar, where she herself would be stationed. There, she drew a parallelogram with a smaller circle inside and a crescent moon inside that—an eye with a crescent moon for a pupil. She added four stars, one in each cardinal direction, to help channel the energies. The pictogram represented the Shadow Realm, the gate from which her Magick flowed. She would tap into it to balance the power between the Oracles.

"Please, Oracles, take your places." Holly directed them with her paw. The Oracles had performed many readings without her, but those were done at the Archway of Apala, where the aquamarine stones acted as a channel. Without them, Holly would be the balancing medium. "I will amplify your gifts," she said. "The reading will be longer and perhaps more detailed, and you may experience more vibrant images or emotions. Even the prophecy itself may be longer in duration I do not know each Oracle pairing is different. I have not experienced a reading with the two of you. Let images come, do not fight them. I will hold your hand, but remember to keep the other on the prophecy stone. Please, let us call the energies. We need to begin."

Perched on the altar, Holly took her place at the top of her symbol, then outstretched a paw to each Oracle.

Together they created their triumvirate of power. They inhaled and exhaled, aligning their energies, and chanted in unison:

> *"Blessed moon, lend us the power of Sight.*
> *Let us see as far as your rays that glisten*
> *and dance upon the earth*
> *For as the light is blocked, we can see all which is hidden.*
> *Humbly, we call to thee; the energy allows us to see.*
> *With open hearts and open minds, we come to thee—*
> *Let your power fill us, be our guide, speak your words.*
> *So mote it be."*

Lady Zarya shuddered. It was her turn to ask for her message:

> *"The time is near; there is nothing to fear.*
> *I am open to the new dawn.*
> *Speak your truth; weave your words.*
> *I am connected to your energy.*
> *I am the Wind, the Fire, the Water, the Earth.*
> *You are the grace by which the elements are peaceful.*
> *You are the strength by which the elements can destroy.*
> *Use me as your tool; deliver your message,*
> *for your wisdom is beyond the ages.*
> *It has traveled the cosmos; it is power over self, over death.*
> *You do not demand anything but my body in this moment,*
> *which I give freely to you.*
> *Walk between two worlds, speak in the stillness of the stars,*
> *and whisper in the birth of planets.*
> *Share with me your message."*

Lady Zarya began to glow, and what started as a soft silver illumination became a blinding light that emanated from her eyes. She raised her hand, still clasping Holly's paw, in the air; light grew from their entwined hands. A breeze played in Lady Zarya's hair but, the curtains remained unmoving. Rain fell inside the room, just outside their circle. The candles burst into flames as the floor quaked beneath their feet. Holly's teeth clenched. She could feel the power surge and the prophecy coming.

Holly's eyes closed as the Dark Fae Oracle's entire body was bathed in silver light. "Rowan, turn away! She is about to speak the prophecy; it will blind you."

Holly knew that to gaze upon the luminosity from an Oracle prophecy reading was dangerous. Human Oracles had caused some damage since they were imbued with the cosmic energy. However, a Fae Oracle could handle large amounts of energy, and these two Oracles were very strong. The damage they could cause to an onlooker would at minimum be temporary blindness, if not permanent issues.

Lady Zarya began to speak. Her voice was strained at first, but after a few moments she took on an ethereal tenor, as if she were speaking from the edge of the universe:

"A child of Light and Dark will unite the courts.
She alone can undo what was done. Her darkness is a
weapon, her light is her shield, and her humanity is her
armor. She will need a guide to walk the path; a warrior or
fool, only she can choose."

The letters materialized and hung in the air, forming each word of the prophecy, dancing around her like cherry blossoms caught in a spring breeze. When Lady Zarya was finished speaking, the words encircled her left hand and crept up her arm, alternating colors from silver to the rainbow of the Chakras. They dipped into her skin, crawling under her flesh. Even shrouded beneath her cloak, the words glowed until they appeared at the top of her right hand. She slapped her hand upon the prophecy stone, the words exploded from her fingertips and twisted into an unrecognizable symbol to anyone other than a Dark Fae. As the symbols were engraved upon the smooth surface, Lady Zarya glowed brighter, and her breathing grew ragged.

"Hold on, Lady Zarya. It is almost over," Holly called out to her.

"Yes," the Oracle said in an exhausted voice. She peeled her raw fingertips away from the stone. They were bloody; and pieces of flesh remained fused to the stone. Holly cracked one eye open and looked upon the gruesome sight. She also knew better than to comfort Zarya.

Lady Sybella picked up where Zarya left off, her smooth voice drowning out the Dark Oracle's ragged breathes. Sybella immediately began her chant:

"I come with an open heart to be filled
with your voice and wisdom.
I do not fear what I shall hear.
You whispered to me before birth and will
when I am on the edge of Oblivion.
In this moment, I am connected to you.
I am the leaves on your tree, the petals on your flower,
the feather on your wings.
Say the words and it shall be done.
I welcome your transformation through Fire that burns.

Wash it away through Water, carry the message in the
Air, and strengthen my path upon the Earth.
I sit in stillness as a child of Light and welcome
the serenity of the darkness.
I wait for you to speak and fill me with
your divine guidance, blessed from the cosmos."

Lady Sybella raised her right hand, and she glowed with a golden light almost instantaneously a silver outline touched the edges, a reminder the prophecy was courtesy of Mother Luna. Her message came rapidly and with no consideration for Sybella's readiness. It was a continuation of Lady Zarya's, though only the two of them would know both prophecies; once this moment passed, they could not reveal the other half to anyone. If they tried, only a stream of unintelligible words would pour from their mouths, a magickal gag. This was a safety measure, so that they would never be at risk of being kidnapped for the other court's prophecies. It was also why it was imperative both courts had a representative present during a reading.

Tears sprang from Sybella's eyes, and her voice took on the otherworldly quality Zarya's had during her reading:

"Today, the moon has eclipsed the sun.
Darkness has won for now.
One light source can show you the way
and yet darken your path.
A child of Light and Dark will appear and shine to lead.
She alone will show that darkness will
not reign in the court forever."

Lady Sybella's eyes glowed a bright amber, and the words she spoke swirled around her, transferring to her stone just as they had with the Dark Oracle.

A bumping and thumping sound came from the corner of the room, and books fell from the bookshelf. Rowan sniffed the air, just as a young Fae boy stumbled forward, tears streaming down his face. The Little One tried covering his eyes, but it was far too late. Holly glanced over her shoulder with one eye blinking open for a quick second, she cried out, trying to warn the boy to hide his eyes to avoid further damage. She knew he had been exposed to the Oracle's light.

The crying boy tried to cover his eyes, but he was in so much pain that he fell forward on his hands and knees. Holly could not disconnect from the Oracles. Sybella was still channeling the energy as the prophecy transferred to stone.

"Rowan, can you get to him?" Holly called over the commotion.

"Is she still glowing?" Rowan asked.

"Yes."

"I can find him by scent, I think." He put his nose to the air.

"Please try, Rowan. The power is not letting up."

A pain-filled cry erupted from the boy, sounding as if lava had been poured into his eyes. Rowan heard the little Fae's rapid breathing and carefully followed the sound as he inched closer to the child.

Rowan could smell his fear. "I am not going to hurt you, Little One, but I cannot have you running around bumping into things. Can we both agree to sit with each other until the Oracles are done with their show?" He heard the little Fae whimper. "My eyes are shut and mind reading, is not one of my gifts, so you will have to answer for me, chap."

"Yes, sir. But my eyes hurt so much," a strained, small voice whispered.

Rowan chuckled. "No, my little friend, I am no sir. Rowan will do fine. What shall I call you?" There was another sniffle, and Rowan moved forward so that the Little One could touch his fur. A soft hand reached for the fox and clumsily hugged his neck. Rowan could feel his tears. The poor thing was scared and in pain, a horrible combination. He leaned into the little Fae to acknowledge the hug.

"My friends call me E."

"Then I would be honored to call you E."

E giggled a little through his tears and gave a sniffly hiccup. This made Rowan smile.

A shriek from Holly ripped through the air, bringing his attention back to the middle of the room.

Chapter Eleven:
PICK A CARD, ANY CARD...

Rowan dared not open his eyes, but the urge was killing him. Facing away from the Oracles, he squinted his eyes open. The power in the room was far from letting go; in fact, the wind seemed to be getting stronger. His hackles rose and his ears pricked up. *Bloody hell, that cannot be a good sign.* He glanced at the floor and realized the light had dimmed further, but they had already passed totality. *Why is it getting darker? It should be getting lighter.* He desperately wanted to turn and look at Holly but could not risk it. Rowan knew something was about to happen.

"E, you must trust me," he said. "I am going to put you back where you were hiding so I can help Holly. I need you to stay there, my friend, until I tell you it is all clear. Do you understand me?"

"Yes, Rowan."

"That's a good chap, hold on." Rowan picked him up by his shirt, placed the boy back in the corner by the bookcase, and slid a floor vase toward him to conceal the boy. He wasn't sure how things were going to play out, and if

Rowan needed to attend to the Oracles first, E might have to wait. *Best to plan and hope it won't come to that.* His gut was telling him to hide the Little One. Rowan opened one eye enough to see the Oracles' glow had faded, but he did not expect what he saw.

Holly and the Oracles were all still bound together, but now parchment papers swirled around the Oracles' hands, shredding into long strips and then into pieces slightly bigger than playing cards. The Oracles raised their hands, and the papers followed, dancing above their heads. Each Oracle radiated intense light from their eyes. As they extended their arms upward, the Oracles' sleeves fell back, and Rowan could see symbols moving under their skin much like the way the words shifted during the prophecy reading.

Rowan backed up, trying to follow the papers as they zipped around. He had never seen a prophecy reading like this. "Holly, what in the worl—?" He lurched forward, the question forgotten, when the symbols exploded out of the Oracles' hands. When the symbols found a home on the paper cards, fleeting images appeared before disappearing in plumes of smoke. The cards danced around the Oracles. A paper floated over Lady Sybella's head, and Rowan could not help but notice the image on it resembled E, while the one floating over Lady Zarya's head bore a striking resemblance to King Jarvok's Lieutenant Asa.

"Holly, what is happening?" Rowan called to her, but 'her face twitched and strained as she channeled the sudden surge of power.

Another card freed itself from the cyclone and hovered on Lady Sybella's side, as did another for Lady Zarya. Holly ignored Rowan's calls—she needed to focus. Her black eyes concentrated on the images displayed on each piece, searching for a pattern.

An additional card appeared over Sybella's head. This one featured a blond Fae, slight with large clear blue eyes, holding these very cards up by her face. A new card rose above Zarya's head too: the image was not of a Fae but of a road or path, Holly could not be sure. The next card was a red chrysanthemum with a young Fae girl's face hiding behind it. The card now over Zarya' represented each of the four elements. A current of energy escaped from the Oracles' bound hands. Purple light unraveled from their hands and stretched to their cards, arching from Sybella's to Zarya's.

The cards glowed, and as they did, a new card from each cyclone through the center. The one from Sybella's side was a sun; Zarya's was the moon. The cards ripped in half and knit themselves back together. A new card formed from the two halves, depicting a crescent moon superimposed on the sun. Two additional cards joined in. Holly caught her breath as she recognized the images: they were of her and Rowan.

"We are all connected. Somehow, we are all connected to this," Holly murmured, scenarios running through her head.

A voice called to her. It sounded like a thousand doves' wings, a moonbeam, and the twinkling of stars all wrapped in velvet. *"Yes, Hecate. You are all intertwined."*

Holly looked around. *"Mother Luna?"* she whispered in her head. She did not want to alarm Rowan in case he could hear her, though the wind drowned out most of the sound. Mother Luna spoke to her directly inside her heart and mind. Holly knew better than to answer with her lips.

"Yes, it is I, Hecate. I am always with you. The Oracles will receive another message. It is for you and Rowan. Pay attention, for what is coming is a long and arduous journey that will affect the future of all the realms. Some of the Fae are noble. Some are not. These Little Ones are the key to the prophecy. They are the Fae who will determine the fate of the realms. You and Rowan must guide them, and sacrifices will have to be made. Remember Hecate, you and Rowan know more than any creature. Death is never the end; it is a transformation of self."

Mother Luna's velveteen voice disappeared, and Holly found herself longing to hear it again. She opened her eyes to find she was crying. Tears dampened her fur. It had been so long since Mother Luna spoke to her or called her by her real name. It was like walking in the sunlight after a year of rain, and Holly did not want to go back to a cloudy sky. But she could not get lost in her thoughts. She had a job to do.

The Oracles began to glow, the veins in their hands lighting up in shades of blue, green, pink, and purple. Holly watched as the energy writhing under their skin transformed into symbols—moon glyphs, she noted to herself. The symbols contorted into words as they traveled across their faces before they simultaneously opened their mouths to speak:

"Kephri, he shall be, and breathe life where it was stolen.
His journey is long and arduous.
Many times, he will feel it is a Herculean effort to complete.
False idols will lead him down the wrong path.
But fear not, Loki is not behind his falls;

he will see through the trickery and
be as swift as Artemis' arrow.
Once his goal is attained, only Cassandra
will understand his pain.
He must stay the course and let Death
walk beside him to escort him home with
the prophecy stone to allow all to atone.
A wind rider becomes a reader, and a healer becomes a leader,
his friend in blood shall be.
The three with Death shall walk into the Veil once more,
along with a new warrior, prepared for war.
Light and Dark will make their final mark."

The cards lit up as each piece of the reading they represented was spoken. Holly took mental notes as Mother Luna had instructed. There was one final surge of power, and the Oracles collapsed, exhausted, along with Holly. Rowan screamed and ran to Holly's side.

The doors burst open. Bishop Geddes stood with four of the Royal Guard. The guards assessed the situation and moved to help the Oracles, but Bishop Geddes shot his right hand out to block them.

"Where are the prophecy stones?" he spat, scanning the room.

Rowan ignored the bishop. "We need help. The Oracles require attention from the Healers. They just finished their reading, and they have collapsed."

The guards looked to each other uncertainly. A smooth voice echoed in Rowan's head: *"Gather the cards, my fox. Do not let the bishop see them. Now, Rowan! Before he notices them."* A stiff breeze drifted through the room. A sheaf of blank parchment blew toward the bishop's face while the cards congregated closer to the fox. Rowan didn't hesitate.

Rowan snatched up the cards and hid them in his vest as the bishop fought off the blank parchment papers. Geddes finally pulled his staff out and twirled it above his head, causing a crystal rock partition to form in front of the open balcony doors, quelling the draft. He fixed his hair and straightened his cloak, then glared at the fox.

"*Stay strong, my Rowan. Mother Luna is with you,*" the voice said.

"What can I do for you, muffin?" Rowan asked the bishop, giving him a toothy grin.

"What did you call me?" Geddes stalked toward the fox.

"Muffin. It is a term of endearment, chap. Like sweetie or honey. Um ... chaps, can you please attend to the Oracles? We should get them some water and perhaps call the healer."

Bishop Geddes's face reddened. "You do not give the orders, fox! Guards, do not move."

But the guards were already at the Oracles' sides, and Holly was making her way toward Rowan. Bishop Geddes' face was pinched with anger. He pushed past Rowan, making a beeline for Holly. Rowan put himself between the bishop and the Dark Oracle's Familiar. He dipped his head low, arched his body and his ears flattened against his head. His bushy tail swayed.

"I want the prophecy stone," Geddes demanded. His eyes turned a stormy grey-green color, the scent of damp stone and moss filling the room. Oh yes, Geddes was angry. Rowan glanced at Holly, a look of confusion passing between them. Technically Bishop Geddes had a claim to the Court of Light's prophecy stone if Queen Sekhmet gave him permission to act as an emissary, but that had not been established before the reading. "I want both stones now. Lady Zarya will write the Dark Fae's prophecy down, or she does not leave," he said.

Rowan gave a low, throaty growl.

The guards froze.

The mink's dark eyes met the unspoken challenge. "You have no claim, nor do you have the right to hold Lady Zarya. She is under no obligation to translate the prophecy unless as ordered by King Jarvok. You have no say, bishop."

Geddes' eyes flicked to the stone on the floor. Holly lunged for the prophecy stone, but it was the size of a dinner plate—once she had the disc in her paws, maneuvering was difficult. While she had speed, Geddes had reach.

Bishop Geddes raised his staff over his head. Rowan was ready to pounce on the bishop, teeth bared, when an Elestial Blade met the staff inches from Holly's body, the reflection of the auric blade turning Holly's black fur white. Geddes yelped to see Asa with her weapon glowing. She parried the staff and sent the bishop sailing backward. Her blue eye was bright like the angry sea while her white eye resembled a blizzard.

"How dare you try to hurt my court's Familiar!" Asa's outrage filled the room like a balloon, pushing everyone backward from the center of the commotion.

The bishop rushed Asa, who redirected him around her body and sent the bishop sprawling clumsily into the chairs, his cape flopping over his head. One of the guards snickered. Snarling, Geddes fought to get his cape off his head. The pungent aroma of wet stone grew twice as strong as before. Geddes was attempting to call his elemental power.

Asa pointed her energetic blade at him as he stood, the weapon popped and sizzled with her anger, "You have no claim to the stone, and if you call your power, I will see it as a direct threat and end you right here."

Bishop Geddes decided to take a more political approach. He looked at the guards. "You saw her try to strike me down, and she threatened me! It is punishable by death. Arrest her!" He jabbed his staff in her direction, its tree agate crystal top winking at her as if it was waiting for him to call upon it. However, no one moved a muscle.

Asa smirked as Desdemona arrived with Nightshade close behind her. Nightshade took a defensive posture a breath behind, allowing her captain to take the lead. Bishop Geddes changed his demeanor yet again. "Captain, thank the universe! This Dark Fae tried to kill me in an unprovoked attack. Order the guards to arrest her!"

Desdemona surveyed the room, which was in utter disarray. The guards tended to the Oracles, who though unconscious seemed to be breathing smoothly and were not in distress. She flicked her eyes to the Familiars, who looked shaken, while Asa appeared nonchalant. That left Geddes; he cringed under her gaze.

"Lieutenant Asa?" Desdemona asked.

Asa shrugged. "Think what you want, Desdemona. He tried to strike my court's Familiar. I merely defended her, as is my right. I am leaving with my Oracle. Your queen promised me safe passage. I am taking Lady Zarya, Holly, and the prophecy stone as my king commanded me. You can try to stop me, but based on the false accusations I have endured, I do not need much more of a reason to fight." Asa glanced over her shoulder, whistled, and Yanka appeared, hovering over the balcony. "Holly, can you make it to Yanka?"

"Yes, I can."

"Good, take the stone and mount up," Asa said, but her eyes never left Desdemona, challenging her former comrade to stop her. Asa's usual decorum and respect were gone after Geddes' attempt on Holly's life. She retrieved the stone from Holly, after noticing the mink wobble with it, out of the corner of her eye.

Geddes lurched forward. "Tell your guards to stop her. Grab the stone!" he yelled, but it was Desdemona who put her hand out now, stiff-arming the bishop. She shoved him backward.

"I cannot, bishop," the Illuminasqua captain said. "They are no longer under my authority, remember? And since I am sure you already asked them and they did not listen to you, it means Lieutenant Asa speaks the truth. You tried to strike Holly down."

Instead of responding, Bishop Geddes reached for Holly, but Desdemona grabbed his cloak and pulled him back. "Go Asa, you have safe passage," Desdemona said as she nodded to the guards to help Lady Zarya onto the dragon. Asa assisted Holly onto Yanka.

The mink and fox exchanged a glance.

Asa gave a subtle tilt of her chin to her former comrade and departed.

The bishop stood again, breathing heavily. "You will pay dearly for that. You stupid troll's ass. Now we do not know what the Dark prophecy was. You are a worthless Power Ang—"

Before he could finish his tirade, Desdemona grabbed him by the throat. "Leave us, now!" she hissed to the rest of the room.

Bishop Geddes flailed in her grip, and Rowan cleared his throat. "Well, blokes, let's say we get Lady Sybella to her room." He snapped his fingers.

The guards followed him without a word or a backward glance to their former captain.

Rowan paused in the threshold. "We already lost a good one today. Do not make it two." He closed the door with his tail.

Desdemona waited for the click before she spoke. "I have dealt with you and your small-minded thinking about my former life for far too long, Geddes. I am not your hired hand. I do not carry out the tasks you are too much of a coward to do yourself. I am not to be trifled with, but for some reason you need reminding of that." She squeezed tighter, and he struggled in her grasp.

"You are nothing," he grumbled even as it became harder to breathe, his windpipe compressing under her pressure.

Impishly, Desdemona curled her lips. "Which means I have nothing left to lose." Her voice was barely above a whisper. Her Elestial Blade unsheathed, the glow illuminating the malevolent look on her face.

Nightshade stepped out from the shadows, removing her black hood. "Captain, please do not do this." Her voice was calm and steady but resonated with strength. Desdemona maintained pressure on the bishop's throat, watching the veins in his forehead budge and his face redden.

"He is not worth it. He is not worthy of your light. We need you to lead us—to show us that our time under

Aurora was not wasted. You still have an oath to fulfill to her and to your kin," Nightshade pleaded.

Desdemona blinked, the rage in her blood receding like the sea after a storm. She glanced over her shoulder.

Nightshade knew the last part of her statement had cut through the angry haze. "Loyalty to the kin," she whispered again.

Desdemona dropped Bishop Geddes, who coughed, clutching his neck. A circle of fingerprints inflamed his skin. "I will see you thrown into the cells for this!" he said, still gasping for air.

Nightshade kicked his foot to draw his attention upward as her captain spoke. "You will do no such thing," Desdemona said, looking down at him. "You threatened the Dark Oracle and her Familiar, which is a punishable offense. The Oracles are neutral Fae; to threaten one means we must turn over the defendant to the Oracle's ruling monarch. I believe King Jarvok will ask for your head. He isn't exactly fond of you."

"You—you would never do that."

Nightshade smiled and pinched his right cheek. "Oh, please try us." She searched his eyes, relishing the glaze of fear. "As officers of the Illuminasqua, we are sworn to enforce the laws of both Oracles because of their neutrality. To threaten them—or their Familiars—falls within our purview, and therefore, we must uphold the law. If you don't leave. We will make good on that. Do not even think of retaliating against our captain, Bishop Geddes, or you will see just how stealthy the Illuminasqua can be. We know you are hiding something, and we will find out what." Nightshade pulled up her hood and, in a blink of an eye, she was gone.

Geddes scrambled to his feet, looking around for Nightshade, but saw only the wide-open door. He ran through it, his footsteps echoing down the hall.

Desdemona closed the door. "Thank you, Illuminasqua." Her protégé reappeared and removed her hood. "The disappearing act was a nice touch. Place Illuminasqua around Lady Sybella's room. I do not trust Geddes to leave her alone."

After Nightshade disappeared again, Desdemona surveyed the room, her boots crunching on the pieces of a broken vase. The furniture was overturned. The drapes had been ripped from the walls, and the altar lay on its side. She inspected the symbols drawn on the floor. The white powder scattered around was soft, a fine ash with no grit. The scent was sage but with a note of cinnamon. *Magickal residue, not usually found after a prophecy reading. That is odd.* Desdemona dusted her fingers off and studied the room. She noticed square outlines on the floor in the Magickal residue, but she could not understand how they were not disturbed. *By the looks of the rest of the room, the residue should have been smeared halfway through the Veil.* Desdemona stroked her chin, contemplating the situation, then bent down to examine the floor. The squares imprints, she noticed, were not clean—the outer corners were broken as if whatever made the marks was picked up in a hurry. She turned toward the bookcase, which was still standing upright; that was puzzling too, considering almost all the furniture was upended.

Before she could scrutinize it any further, Ora and Orion burst into the room, swords and spears drawn. Without thinking, Desdemona dragged her foot through the squares remaining on the floor. She wasn't sure if it was a reflex or something more profound, but a voice from somewhere deep inside told her to subtly scuff the lines with her boot, and she listened without hesitation. By the time she was nose-to-nose with Orion, there was no more evidence. "Orion, Ora. The Oracles finished their reading as I arrived. The room was in shambles when I got here." She stepped aside so they could survey it for themselves. Desdemona knew the House of Hathor's guards—and especially the twins—were very suspicious by nature.

The two exchanged a glance. "The queen asked us to check on the Oracles. We heard a commotion and saw Bishop Geddes leaving, somewhat upset." Orion's eyes narrowed.

Desdemona smiled. "When is he not upset about something?" She casually waved her hand. "He thought someone was deliberately trying to keep him from the reading. He came in complaining about it, ridiculous really. Imagine someone trying to keep the bishops from a prophecy reading." Her voice held a challenge.

Ora caught on. "How dare you! The queen did no such thing!" she spat, her quietness melting away. Orion put his arm on his twin's shoulder. He knew what Desdemona was trying to do.

"I did not say anything about the queen, Ora." Desdemona walked past the two guards. "Feel free to inspect the room. I have a few items in need of my attention."

Ora gave a curl of her lips, more of a growl, but remained silent until the door shut behind Desdemona. "Stupid. I deserve a lashing. Forgive me, brother. I broke the basic Vila code. You are my senior and witnessed my weakness." She handed him a gilded leather whip from her belt. The handle had the House of Hathor tree with green jade and tiger's eye stones set into the design. The whip itself was made of leather with thick braided tails. In the center were seven smaller tails, compact and bundled together for maximum coverage. She dropped her body armor and exposed her bare back; gnarled skin and scars twisted across her ebony skin. As the light caught her skin, it glittered as if it was dusted with the finest gold, milled to a soft powder and woven into her cells. She stood tall and straight.

Orion nodded and accepted the honor of punishing his sister. "For every mistake we make, we must learn, and the scars are a reminder of such. Let these scars be the bark of the tree. You shall not break under the pain. You shall not bend under the pressure. You shall not cry under the agony, but instead, grow taller. Let your roots ground you to the House of Hathor, and so you shall learn from your mistakes. With every lash, may you grow a new branch, sprout a new leaf. As your blood flows, know it flows for your mistake, and you will not let it happen again. It will act as a reminder to only speak when it is necessary and not from emotion. That is your lesson, dear sister. Your lashing for this mistake is seven. Your cleansing must be whole and complete."

Ora took a breath. "I accept my punishment, dear brother. I shall only speak when it is necessary. I shall control my emotions. I am a stronger warrior than my emotions. All for the House of Hathor, my honor as a Vila warrior, and my queen. Cleanse me of my weakness, so mote it be."

Orion hoisted his arm and began inflicting her lesson. He would not take pity on her. She was silent and did not flinch as the leather snapped at her skin, as blue blood followed the curve of her spine. After the seventh blow, Orion whipped the leathers to the side to wipe away the blood and the bits of flesh clinging to the tool. He returned it to Ora with both hands and bowed. She thanked him and put her armor back on. She did not cover the wounds or acknowledge them.

"Let us return to the queen," Orion said.

Chapter Twelve:
CHANGE OF PLANS

T he wind on Zarya's skin was cool. She lay with her cheek pressed against the creature's neck, her breath a constant, steady rhythm. Her cloak had fallen back during their ascent, and her hair whipped behind her and hit Asa with each dip and turn the dragon took.

Holly curled up at the nape of Zarya's neck, trying to keep her ward comfortable. Lady Zarya still felt a bit clammy. "I am worried about her falling ill," the mink yelled back to Asa, who rode with her arms protectively circled around Zarya.

Asa waved Zarya's loose braid out of her face. "We will get her to a healer. I believe she is exhausted from the reading."

Holly unfurled herself as the Oracle stirred underneath her. Zarya's breathing deepened. Relief washed over the mink. Zarya was regaining consciousness.

"You are safe, Lady Zarya. We are returning to Blood Haven," Asa said in a calm, reassuring voice, but there was

an edge of anger, probably left over from Bishop Geddes's aggression toward Holly.

The Oracle's eyes opened wide. "No! Wait, please, you can't—you do not understand, we must go back!" Lady Zarya's voice was hoarse from the reading.

Asa shook her head. "I have direct orders from King Jarvok to return you to Blood Haven."

"No! No! Stop! Halt!" Zarya thrashed and kicked Yanka's sides.

Holly had never seen Zarya act like this before, but she had witnessed enough Magick in her time to know when to listen. She had a hunch this had something to do with the cards; she recognized the Oracles had firsthand knowledge as conduits of the Magick. The Oracles, she understood, had likely seen something in those cards that she and Rowan had not.

"Land this creature now!" Zarya commanded, her voice ringing with power and authority. She turned to face the Dark Fae. "Please, Asa, this has to do with you, the prophecy, and our kin's survival."

Yanka reared and lurched in the air. Asa could tell the dragon was frustrated at being kicked by the Oracle.

Asa had not yet pierced the second layer of the Veil, which meant they were still in the Court of Light's domain and not far from the palace. Her brows pinched at the thought of landing close to the palace. "Yanka, find us a place to land with coverage, please." The Ice-Breather snorted in response and headed toward the Forehelina Forest. The thick lilac flowers of the two-hundred-foot trees would be in full bloom and provide ample coverage. "Once we land, you will have less than an infant Will-o-Wisp's light to tell me what is going on before I throw you over my shoulder and take you back to Blood Haven. Do we understand each other, Lady Zarya?" Asa said.

The Oracle nodded and her shoulders relaxed. Yanka banked left and began her descent. The dragon expertly navigated through the canopy of thick, fragrant lilac blooms and branches, tucking and rolling her wings to help slow their speed. She was the only dragon that could have maneuvered through the dense forest so well. Yanka closed her wings to fit through the smallest opening, causing a quick acceleration of their fall, but then unfurled them in time to float to the ground

Asa dismounted first to scan the area. Once she was confident it was clear, she nodded for everyone to follow, but not before she gave Yanka a rub on her snout for her skillful flying. The dragon pushed her nose into her rider's hands.

Asa gave her hand to Lady Zarya and helped her to a fallen log to sit. Holly hopped down and tagged along.

"Well? What is this all about?" Asa folded her arms across her chest, her patience wearing very thin. Lady Zarya straightened her cloak.

Holly curled up into her ward's lap. "Please tell us. I—" She stared at Zarya's face. "Your eyes! Lady Zarya, you have been gifted! Asa, look!" Startled, the Oracle stood, knocking Holly off her lap, but the mink was far too agile to be injured. She twisted nimbly in midair and landed on her feet.

"What?" Asa asked.

"Look at her eyes, her pupils!" Holly exclaimed, practically hopping from paw to paw in excitement.

Zarya backed up as Asa tried to get closer, suddenly afraid.

Asa grabbed the Oracle by her wrists.

"What is it?" Zarya winced as Asa examined her face, she leaned in, nose to nose with the Oracle. She tried backing away, but Asa held tightly to the Oracle's wrists.

"What in the universe?" Asa mumbled, leaning in.

"What is it?" Lady Zarya attempted pulling away. Her eyes watered with unshed tears, her body shaking as Asa held her. "Please tell me ... am I cursed?"

"No, this is a gift from the universe," Holly said, but she could not tell Zarya she was marked by Mother Luna, and most likely Lady Sybella was as well. When the Oracles died, they would be met by Mother Luna and given another chance as a Familiar, like Rowan. They would be claimed by the Shadow Realm. Their gift of sight and prophecy had been heightened, that was why today's reading was so unusual. She and Rowan had succeeded in their mission. "Your pupils bear the gift of sight. Your right one is now in the shape of a star and the left one is in the shape of a crescent moon, representing the Court of Dark. It is because of the new reading today. You have been gifted, Lady Zarya, with another way to read, an additional level to your power. Blessed be." Holly dropped upon her knees, and Lady Zarya did the same they both held each other, hand to paw.

"Blessed be to the energies which deem myself and Sybella worthy of such wisdom. So mote it be."

Holly stood and kissed each eyelid. "You must share what you saw with Asa. Rowan took the picture cards, and now, after seeing your eyes, I believe this has to do more with that than the prophecy stone."

Lady Zarya gathered her composure and sat down once more as Holly took her place on her lap, wanting to be petted. "Yes, Holly, the image cards play a large part in this."

Asa could no longer stay quiet. "What image cards?"

Lady Zarya put a delicate hand to her heart. "Lieutenant Asa, forgive me. This has been a most unusual day, and I apologize for my panicked response. The reading had unforeseen developments."

"Unforeseen developments in a prophecy reading," Asa said with pursed lips.

Holly interjected for the sake of time. "After the Oracles received their prophecy, another message came through via a different modality."

Asa shrugged. "And?"

Lady Zarya pulled out a small rectangular piece of parchment and handed it to her.

The Dark Fae took it slowly. There was a septagram scorched into the front of the paper, and when she turned it over, she saw the image of a Fae boy between six and eight years old. "Do we know his faction?"

Holly and Zarya glanced at each other.

"No, Lieutenant, why?" Holly asked.

Asa rubbed her temples. "Because his age is hard to decipher without knowing his faction. If he is tied to a flora or fauna group, that will affect how he matures. He is obviously an Earthborn Fae, so that is another factor. He could be twelve earth years but appear to be only six."

Holly nodded in understanding. "Do the Light Fae celebrate their earth years?"

"Yes," Zarya said. "Much like the humans celebrate birthdays. Aurora set the protocol of celebrating when they took the moniker of Fae as a way of marking the end of their angelic lineage while Earthborn Fae celebrate their naming day."

Asa shook her head. "I have been reborn at least three times now, as an Angel, a Power Angel, and a Dark Fae. I don't need a celebration every time."

Holly cleared her throat.

"Right, let's get back to the task at hand instead of debating the Light Fae's frivolous traditions." Asa looked at the card again. The child was striking, almost beautiful, she noted. His cheeks were babyish. His medium brown hair reached just past his chin, a striking silver streak originating from the left side of his temple. His eyes were a stunning amber hue with a navy-blue ring around the iris. They were full of wisdom, depth, and innocence. She looked closer and noticed his right eye was crying a single tear. The word DEATH was written at the bottom of the tear. Asa ran her finger across the jagged edge of the parchment from where the cards had ripped during their creation.

A chill ran through her. "So, what does this mean?" Asa asked, holding the parchment aloft.

"He was present during the readings," Zarya said.

Asa took her helmet off and raised it as if she was going to throw it. "A Little One was present for the readings? When no other Fae heard them during an eclipse?"

"I knew the Fae was there during the reading, but I was a bit indisposed at the time. Rowan hid the Little One for his protection. Hopefully they haven't found him," Holly admitted.

"So, you know what he looks like? How tall he is? Pertinent details?" Asa asked.

Holly grimaced. "Not exactly, my eyes were closed."

"Does Rowan?" Asa asked her voice sounding impatient

"His eyes were closed too, but he spoke to him," Holly answered with her paw raised as if that was a victory.

Asa scowled and tapped her foot. "And when exactly were you going to mention that a Light Fae witnessed the prophecy reading?"

The Oracle and the mink looked at each other and shrugged. "Asa, it was chaotic, to say the very least," Holly said. "Lady Zarya was unconscious, and I did not want to mention the Fae in front of Geddes."

Asa looked like she was ready to explode. Her hands clenched, her jaw tight, and her white eye sparking with power, she was inches away from losing it.

"Lieutenant, before you get all worked up, can I just explain—" Zarya began.

Holly opened her mouth to assist Zarya in her explanation but, Yanka intervened, circling her tail around the Dark Fae to hug her. The dragon leaned her neck against her rider, letting her cool breath calm her rider. "Thank you, my little love," Asa murmured, kissing the dragon's snout. With an exhale, she placed her helmet back on. "Continue with your explanation, Zarya," a visibly calmer Asa urged, while Yanka stayed close by. But still her eye sparked every now and then, making Holly jump.

Zarya gave a close-lipped nod. "We need to go back for him. I am afraid for his life. I believe the new queen will kill him—or worse. Surely, the bishops will send him to his Oblivion because he knows both prophecies and about the cards." Holly placed her paw over Lady Zarya's hand.

"Why is this so important, how is it all connected?" Asa's voice grew gentler.

Lady Zarya knew Asa would need more convincing if she was going to disobey direct orders from King

Jarvok. "The bishops cannot be trusted—we all know they are hiding something. Geddes is intent on getting the prophecy stones. The cards said that this boy is the key to the prophecies and the two courts. If he is captured, this prophecy will never come to fruition. Asa, you are the one I saw in the cards as his guardian. You are meant to walk the path together. The two of you are tied. You must go back and rescue him. There is a voice deep down telling me he is in the cells. By all that is light in the Universe I hope they have not found him. That Fae is in trouble. He is the only Fae who knows both prophecies. Her new eyes focused on Asa's.

"If—and this is a big if—I agree to this, you must return to Blood Haven with Yanka right now. Jarvok said that if you do not return by moonrise, the Blaze Battalion will be discharged to burn the palace to the ground."

Lady Zarya nodded. "Of course. I give you my word."

"Yanka will take you and Holly. There you will tell King Jarvok what you have explained to me and why I have disobeyed him."

Holly spoke up. "I will return with you to the palace."

Asa shook her head in protest, but she was outnumbered.

"I agree," Lady Zarya said. "Holly should accompany you."

Asa exhaled. "I am not winning this argument, am I?"

"I am afraid not, Dark Fae." Holly gave Asa a playful jab.

Zarya chimed in. "Holly and I had not discussed the ramifications of the reading, and she was not privy to the other visions that Sybella and I had. She could not have known."

Holly looked down sheepishly. "Thank you, Zarya, but I did receive a message that the Little One was crucial to the prophecy. I was going to go back myself and deal with it, though I had not made the connection that this particular Fae was the one from the prophecy until you confirmed it."

"You would have gone alone?"

"Yes. I did not want to put you in any more danger."

Zarya hugged the mink. "That is very sweet, Holly."

Asa looked between the two mystical creatures. "Okay, okay, big energies at play, no one handled this particularly well. Let me see if I can sum this up: the Little One snuck in, witnessed the reading, and somehow is the key to this, but no one can tell me why."

Holly nodded.

"Then let's go, Holly. Zarya, I'll handle my end of the bargain," Asa said.

The Oracle mounted Yanka without hesitation. "Are you sure you can make it back on foot?"

Asa smiled. "Yanka was very smart with where she put us. The Forehelina Forest is just outside the palace grounds. It will provide coverage, and there should be a jumping-off point for her to catch some air nearby, even if she needs to follow the Bridge of Oroki and jump from there. Go— King Jarvok is expecting you."

Holly turned to leave but Lady Zarya stopped her with a raise of her hand. placing a necklace around the mink's neck. "For luck."

Holly could not see it—it was more like a collar or choker—but she could tell there was a small charm from the tinkling sound it made when she moved. "Thank you, my lady." Holly bowed her head and touched the Oracle's cheek with her paw. Lady Zarya covered Holly's paw with her own hand, and the two locked eyes in a gentle goodbye

Asa put her forehead to Yanka's, stroking the side of the dragon's face. Yanka's vapor tusks released condensation ribbons. The dragon did not like leaving her rider like this. "Get Lady Zarya home safely. You have my vial to get you through the Veil. I will see you soon, my little love." Asa tugged on the enchanted vial, which held her blood. The dragon pressed her head forward. "My heart melts only for you." She kissed the dragon's nose as Yanka's breath chilled her skin. The dragon clacked her teeth, and when that didn't elicit a response, she whined a bit "What?" Asa asked.

The dragon pressed against Asa, clicking and clacking.

"I have to go, luv. I promise I will be back."

The Ice-Breather's soulful eyes were etched with pain. Holly placed a small paw on the dragon's back leg and patted it.

"What is it with you?" Asa said. "We find the little Fae, and boom, I head back to Blood Haven. Sure, I'll have some explaining to do, but if Lady Zarya does her job, Jarvok will only be his usual amount of troll's prick level mad at me, okay?" She weakly smiled. "Now get going before Jarvok sends the Blaze Battalion to burn everything in their path."

Asa turned to Holly. "Ready?" She bent down to allow Holly to jump on her shoulder and wrap around her neck. They watched as Yanka ran, branches snapping, until she found a place to catch an updraft. The dragon took off, her magenta body breaking through the lilac canopy. The blooms fell around them. Holly inhaled their sweet fragrance.

Asa glanced down at the boy's face on the card. "So, I am searching for a Merfolk scale in an ocean? Well, we better get a move on. Hold on Holly." Asa took off running and vaulting into the deep-purple forest, heading back toward where she had come from, but with a new motive and an unclear future.

Chapter Thirteen:
CRYSTAL CLEAR

J arvok followed the glow of the torches as their light danced on the crystal walls. The wisps of orange cast just enough illumination for him to see how far ahead the group of Light Fae were. This helped him to keep a respectable distance to allow the band their time to grieve. At least that was what he told himself. He knew he was not welcome or wanted. He believed this particular cluster of mourners would turn on him, blaming him for all that had transpired today. However, he had not plunged the blade into her chest, nor had he told her to kill anyone. Though he had selected the mode of execution, Jarvok had his reasons for that, and the mourners would never comprehend them.

King Jarvok was confident every Fae in the Court of Light believed the culpability landed squarely on his scarred shoulders. Some felt that his and Aurora's upcoming union caused a schism inside a very happy kingdom. They believed she crumbled under the pressure, driving a once sane queen mad. Yet others said she was a cunning ruler

who had played him and had never planned to unify the two courts. Another rumor was that she had planned on assassinating him on their Unity night but that someone had found out and forced her hand, making her sloppy.

Regardless of how they had ended up here, he knew it was always a Dark Fae's fault where a Light Fae was concerned. Jarvok found a fissure of crystal and wedged himself in, his armor digging into his sides. He grimaced but, with one final shove, wiggled deeper inside. He wasn't quite sure what he was doing here, but he sensed there was unfinished business.

The cavern was carved from celestite crystal, a sky-blue-hued crystal with a spiritual connection to the crown Chakra. It helped to quiet the mind and ease emotional turmoil. The crystal instilled a sensation of calm to allow mourners to express themselves, helping them to accept and find words of comfort. Pillars inside the catacomb were reinforced with rhodonite, pale-pink and magenta crystal columns with black veins running through them. Rhodonite crystal aided mourners in turning their focus away from those who had met their Oblivion and back toward the living. The crystal reminded them their life had not ended just because their love one's had—the difference between empathy and martyrdom.

The group positioned the body, in its sarcophagus, at the center of the cave; Aurora's place was already cleared. Malascola walked around, carving symbols into the floor. Jarvok watched as the Gnome's gauntlets guided the acid from his skin, creating a precise stream that cut through the crystal as easily as the roar from a dragon would wake a dreamer from the most blissful sleep.

The stocky Fae placed his hand on her sarcophagus, smoke emanating from the seam. *He is sealing it.*

Malascola bowed his head and walked away, patting Theadova's neck as he passed. The Gnome glanced back one last time at Aurora's sarcophagus. Then he tightly shut his eyes. Whether he was trying to remember her or wipe away the memory of Aurora lying in the sarcophagus, he wasn't telling.

The white stag was next. He gave a graceful bow, his hooves sounding hollow on the crystal as he stepped forward and then back again, gathering his fortitude. "Aurora?" His voice cracked. He licked his teeth and swallowed hard.

Jarvok listened, sure he would hear nothing but curses of his name, but that was not what transpired.

"I am so sorry. You were finally happy." Theadova's antlers bloomed and pink blossoms fell with his tears. "I am not sure what happened over these past few weeks. I saw the change in you when Jarvok came, and you let him in."

Oh yes, here it is where you blame me for her downfall.

"Your light was bright, but when he came into your life, it was blinding. I do not know what scared you, but whatever it was, I wish you had trusted us more. I would have helped you, but that is all in the past. Your light led me; it still does. I do not care what they say. He was still what was best for you. I am sorry it ended this way for you, Aurora. You deserved so much better. He did not mean it— do not blame him. Jarvok was hurt. You know he lashes out. We were all confused because you were not yourself. Perhaps we put too much on you. All my love and light, Aurora. I will miss you, my queen. These torches will burn forever just as your light will shine in my heart forever. Goodbye." Theadova bowed and exited the cave, soft pink petals trailing from his gilded antlers, punctuated by the diminishing sound of his hooves.

The metal Gnome with the red beanie hugged the bottom of the casket in silence. Crying, he stood on his tiptoes and placed his red beanie on the lid. "Mes needed one last hugs from yous ... alls mes loves and lights." His gruff voice was strained. He stuffed his oversized hands in the pockets of his blacksmith apron and walked out. Theadova waited for him a safe distance away.

Jarvok swallowed, his rage quelled. It took some effort to lift his hands from his sides. Jarvok ran his fingertips over the smooth, cool crystal walls, hoping for clarity. *What am I doing here? What did I hope to accomplish?* Asa would retrieve Lady Zarya and return her safely to Blood Haven. Dragor was waiting outside the palace grounds to take him home.

Once there, Jarvok would sort out the prophecy readings with Zion, Asa, and the High Council. For now, he had already agreed to share his Oracle's readings, and Sekhmet had agreed to share hers. The treaty was still intact if he left without a confrontation.

I am a Fae of my word. I never said I wouldn't visit her body, and I don't plan to cause a scene—not here. I'll leave as soon as I see her.

Jarvok had seen Yanka leave before he made his way down to the catacombs. Therefore, he had not broken his word, and as far as he knew, Sekhmet had not broken hers.

Jarvok heard the heavy doors shut, leaving him alone with the cool glow of the blue flame torches. He stepped out from the crevice and made his way to the casket. Aurora was the first to be laid in the catacombs, and the emptiness was not lost on him. The cavern seemed more like the gaping jaws of a serpent, with the crystal stalactites and stalagmites playing the part of fangs. He glanced around and noticed honeycombs carved into the walls, most likely so that family members of the monarchs could be laid with them.

The faceted crystal sparkled even in the darkness. He recalled Aurora had spoken of designing the catacombs with Malascola. Lady Serena's influence was involved too. Aurora and Serena had disagreed on whether the Fae had souls: Lady Serena thought they did, but Aurora was not convinced enough to go against their core beliefs. It was a sticking point between the two friends. He remembered Aurora telling him it had sullied one of their last conversations, and it gnawed at her. He could picture the hurt look in her turquoise eyes when she spoke of the mermaid; they turned a paler hue like the light was taken from them. Still beautiful but missing their golden spark.

He found himself looking upward, trying not to let those moments overtake him. Otherwise, he was never going to say what he wanted to. A single ray of light funneled through the ceiling of the cavern—a beacon in the dark catacomb.

Jarvok squinted at the small opening in the ceiling. There was etching around it and along the walls. He unsheathed his Elestial Blade for added light and touched the symbols. The ciphers at eye level were hidden in swirls of leaves and elemental designs, but he figured it out. They were arrows—directions, in fact—pointing to the hole in the ceiling. He put his hand over his mouth to stifle his laughter. If Lady Serena was correct and they did have souls, Aurora had placed directions for the souls to exit the catacombs. "Clever Fae," he with said a smile. He muffled the pride overtaking him. *Why am I smiling?*

"Damn it to Lucifer!" Jarvok spat out, a curse he rarely used after Asa had asked him to strike it from the Dark Fae's vernacular. He marched to the crystal coffin, his anger bubbling to the surface. However, what he saw stopped him yet again.

Chapter Fourteen:
A Dead Body Tells No Tales

J arvok stood over her casket, and his' breath left him, along with his fury and grief. Aurora lay in what resembled tranquil repose. They had changed her gown and cleaned her. All signs of her execution had vanished. The coffin was configured in the shape of her element, Air: a triangle with a bar at the top. It was constructed of clear Elestial quartz with an opal inlay, the milky-white iridescence encased in a pure gold outline. At the top of the coffin was a symbol made of tanzanite, Aurora's companion crystal; it formed a circle with three wavy lines, denoting her faction as the first and only Sylph. The rare violet crystal had been kept secret from the humans due to its scarcity and its powerful ability to easily shift one's consciousness. Jarvok smiled, remembering the elegant piece of tanzanite she wore around her neck. The blue, almost violet, crystal looked gorgeous against her skin, sitting delicately in the hollow if her throat. She would often say the necklace helped her to communicate. He had planned to feature tanzanite in their Unity rings. The scowl returned

to his face with that fleeting thought. *I had many plans for our rings.*

The inside of her casket was lined in pure white silk, a stark contrast to her crimson hair. She was dressed in a blue gown that looked like the ocean, with gold symbols embroidered around the hem, and her arms were folded across her stomach as if she were sleeping. *Though you usually slept on your side with your right leg thrown over mine, and you would steal all the covers. You always said you were cold.* He shook the memory away. He glanced at her face and noticed her crown, swallowing. There was the disc that brought them together. He almost believed that if he tapped on the crystal, she would open those turquoise eyes and smile.

"Illusion," he groaned, and with one word, the anger rushed back like storm clouds overtaking the plains on a summer's day. *Illusions are what the Court of Light is so very good at.* "Love, hope, a place to belong. It was a figment of my imagination, perpetrated by you," he said to the coffin, running his index finger along the edge as he paced. "That was the plan: make me drop my guard, make me believe I could have it all. Why? So that you could control my Weeper Army?" He turned his back to the casket. "Right?" His voice lacked conviction. Their time in the meadow didn't seem like a trick. Jarvok glanced at the body. This was the first time he had been alone with his thoughts, and now he wasn't sure of anything.

The Dark Fae King marched back to the sarcophagus. "You admitted to wanting to kill me! I saw the blade with the iron in it!" he growled, like he was looking for an answer. "I would have done anything for you! All you had to do was ask. I would have slain any monster, walked through fire! No task would have been insurmountable. I would have bled for you. I loved you, Aurora. More than life, I loved you. Why didn't you love me back?"

Jarvok put his head down on the casket, wrapping his arms around the cool crystal, prepared to give into his grief. Instead of crying, he jerked his head up. "Iron? That small amount of iron may not have killed me ... and you were far too careful to take that chance." He paced as his mind worked and massaged his thoughts. "The only sure way to bring about my Oblivion is with an Elestial Blade or a Harbinger blade after an Elestial Strike, like Desdemona did to you." Realization and regret flashed across his face. "Unless you were not planning on killing me with the con-coction in the blade. It would have slowed me down so your dog could do your dirty work. You were going to send Desdemona to finish me off. The iron was to make it easier for Desdemona to kill me." He shook off the seeds of doubt that logic was beginning to sow in his brain.

"No. No! I will not let you do this to me again!" He pivoted and marched up to the casket. "You will not make a fool of me in death, Aurora. I will not allow you to play games with my mind." He pointed at her through the quartz. "You admitted to wanting me dead. I heard it with my own ears. Then you sent me a curse with that note. Sekhmet even warned me before you could enact it. Dragor incinerated it. The note had your seal—I am done!" He picked up the beanie the Gnome had left on the casket and threw it on the floor. Jarvok stared at it. He could practically hear Asa in his head, scolding him for throwing it. Jarvok raised his chin to the ceiling, his shoulders slumping. "Damn it to Lucifer, that was childish of me, but..." Jarvok retrieved the beanie and smoothed it out, placing it back on the edge of the casket.

The king removed an old, weathered pouch from his pocket and carefully laid it on the casket and untied the strings with shaking fingers. Inside were the remains of an angel feather preserved in gold, curved into a C-shape. When he placed it on the crystal, it made a pinging sound like an anvil that had been struck. "This little feather was the only one which survived my fall back to earth, protected by my armor when I tucked it away. No, it wasn't mine. I lost my wings; most fell off on my way back up and whatever I had left burned off when I fell back after they used the Wormwood Trumpet. No, little queen, this does not belong to me." The feather had awoken him on the beach, landing on his face, though he had not known at the time where it had come from. He slid the feather so it was directly over the disc in her crown on the casket.

Jarvok carried it with him as a symbol of his rebirth, a promise that if something so sickly and ugly could be cast aside yet still survive, so could the Power Angels. *That was the start of my true life.* He held it up to the torch light. "You had the disc. I had this." Jarvok closed his fist around the feather. After he found out Aurora had the disc he had given to Serena, Asa had read the feather. She was confident she could determine who it once belonged to.

"It was you, Aurora!" Jarvok threw his hands up. "This feather was yours. To think that all this time, we had a piece of each other, motivating one another, like we were fated by the universe to meet. I was going to give it to you on our Unity Day—have it made into a ring. I thought it was a beautiful gesture. I am a fool!" He squeezed his eyes shut. Until he could feel the skin around them crinkle and move his helmet.

Jarvok shook his head and opened his eyes, regaining his composure. "So, take it back. I don't want it!" But even as he raised his hand to throw the feather, he knew he couldn't bring himself to do it. He lowered his arm. Tears welled beneath his helmet. "You have taken so much from me." Jarvok tucked the gold feather away. So far, only Asa knew the identity of the feather's owner; Jarvok had not even told Zion. "It will stay that way," he whispered, a hitch in his voice on the last word as if he was ashamed or perhaps disappointed that he could not discard the feather.

Jarvok took off his helmet and ran his hands through his hair. His smile was almost unhinged. "I will tell you a little secret since you won't be sharing it with anybody." He pressed his face close to the crystal sarcophagus, causing condensation to form on the clear quartz. "You helped me today. Your death proved a longstanding theory of mine, a secret I have held close to my Elestial Blade." He drew a heart in the vapor. "You always said what a wonderful strategist I am." Jarvok had long thought the story of how Desdemona fought Lucifer was suspicious. *How could a mere Power Angel take that type of beating and survive, much less inflict damage on Lucifer the Light Bringer?* She hadn't just damaged him; she had severed his arm. It was often assumed Michael had channeled his power through her Elestial Blade to help her, but Jarvok had never bought it. Gabriel hadn't had enough time to call Michael.

"I never understood why she was chosen to lure Lucifer or why the Archangel commanders were so sure he would show for her. I began to question them." Jarvok tapped the sarcophagus. A ghost of a smile flickered on his face, as if he was enjoying finally telling someone this secret. "You asked me about the scar on my face. It was courtesy of Desdemona. I confronted her with my suspicions before she was exalted, and let's just say she did not take kindly to my inquiry." He smirked. Before they had finished their rather heated debate, he and Desdemona were separated by Commander Michael. Desdemona was due to be exalted, so she outranked Jarvok; he had received seven lashes in the Hollows for insubordination. The Dark Fae king had fallen in line after the punishment and become the epitome of a proper Power Angel, but he had never forgotten his theory. He had read the texts on what transpired between her and Lucifer; he had wondered about her chosen name. The human translation of Desdemona was "misery" or "ill-fated," but it also included the word *demon*. "I had her kill you because I knew it would prove my theory," he said. "Once I gave the little change in instructions, I saw Asa sway and begin to sweat. Her Kyanite armor should have protected her from emotions that were too strong. The Kyanite grounds us. Negativity slides off. Lucifer is the only creature with enough power to penetrate Kyanite if we are not shielded properly. An empath of Asa's strength can sense the Hellfire in Lucifer's blood." That was why Asa was so special in the brigade; she could warn a platoon of an impending attack. Where other Power Angels would be paralyzed by his rage, she was their early warning system and allowed them to charge their Angelite discs with the Shining Kingdom's Glory before battle so that the Power Angels were not left vulnerable to Lucifer.

Jarvok tapped on the quartz, pointing out the disc in Aurora's crown. A cackle escaped him, and he covered his mouth for a moment. "Lucifer's blood rage could affect an empath such as Asa if she was without her disc. She would sweat, sensing him before an attack, like she was burning in Hell's fires. Because only Lucifer has the rage of Hellfire in his blood—and so do his offspring."

Chapter Fifteen:
BAD TO WORSE

E glanced up when he heard maniacal laughter. "What was that?" He leaned forward, trying to make it out. Whoever it was, their laughing didn't match what they were feeling, as though humor and sorrow had been mixed up. "I hate this place. It doesn't make any sense." E shook his head.

The laughing stopped.

E was not upset over losing his sight; though it aided him in aura reading, he did not need it to know what had transpired. His stomach was in knots over the lies he had heard from the Fae in the room. E knew their colors didn't match their words. The little Fae had sensed Captain Desdemona was going to hurt Bishop Geddes very badly. Her intention was clear, like when a Will-o-Wisp goes out looking for a fight—someone is going to get beat up, that was just how it went. If the other Illuminasqua had not interrupted her, the captain would have sent Bishop Geddes to his Oblivion. The room had boiled when Desdemona was holding the bishop's throat, like someone had started a fire in the room. As soon as she dropped him, it had gone out.

However, there was one moment of quiet amid the squall of emotions. The Dark Fae, the one they called Asa, had defended Holly, but more importantly, when she entered the room, E had felt safe. E's grandmother, Wendoura, had told him that when two aura readers of equal power were together, their auras calmed each other. *Perhaps Asa is an aura reader too.* He had always been taught to fear the Dark Fae, but she had calmed him so much that he had reached out toward her. All he had received back was coldness, like he had opened an empty grave—which made no sense to him.

The part E had hated more than anything was listening as the man in gold hurt the woman who had turned out to be the man's own sister, Ora. However, she had asked him to do it and E could sense she was fine with it. That confused him most of all, as she had not done anything wrong. His momma always told him not to hit another Fae, unless they hit you first and their intention was to cause harm. His father had a different philosophy.

"Hit last and hit the hardest," he had said. E didn't like to hit anyone, so Ora wanting to be punished for speaking puzzled him.

E shook his head, he needed to stop wasting time thinking about silly things. He could no longer wait for Master Rowan to return, he could think about the Dark Fae Asa later once he was home, warm in bed. He had witnessed enough arguments and threats. He knew that if Geddes found out he heard the prophecy he would be thrown in the cells, and he would never see his momma again. *Momma must be so worried.* He wanted to cry, thinking about her, but knew it would make his eyes hurt again. E wasn't sure how much time had passed, but he had to at least try to get out. Though his eyes were burning, his landscape was not complete blackness; a painful blur of light and shape made up his world now. He had not yet allowed his young mind to consider whether this would be his world forever.

E fortified himself. He would not let this break him. His father hated weakness, and E had been on the receiving end of far too many energy smacks for being "a sensitive little Fae," as his father called him. He closed his eyes and centered himself the way his grandmother had taught him. This helped silence the extra emotions swirling around him. E took a breath and crawled forward, pausing after a few feet to listen for voices. There was nothing he could detect by sound, so he reached out with that extra side of him and waited for a response. His grandmother, his Mima, had explained it much like casting a fishing net. E threw his pretend net in front of him, seeing if he could catch any auras or emotions. Nothing flickered in his mind.

The aura reader stayed on his hands and knees as he maneuvered around, trying to picture the room. He did not know what he would do if he managed to escape, but right now he had to concentrate on getting across the floor. He recoiled as he dragged his right knee through shards of ceramic and bumped his shoulder against the altar's table leg. His eyes welled up, but he shut them tight, knowing the pain from crying was not worth the emotional relief a good cry might provide. He would not be pathetic. He had to keep going and get back to his momma, Dora, and Indiga. He had overheard the fighting in the courtyard and hoped they were all okay.

E stretched his arm, his fingers spread wide, trying to feel and circumvent the table. He touched the leg, his face scrunched up as his felt the curved foot—*it's lying on its side*—which confused him even more.

That was when he felt the breeze.

E froze. He fixed his gaze on the door and the gold shape moving toward him, but there was nowhere for him to go.

"A silver streak of diamonds in your hair, Little One," a deep voice above him said. "There is only one way you could have gotten it." The gold silhouette reached down and grabbed E by the scruff of his neck.

Chapter Sixteen:
RUN AND STRIKE A POSE

A sa ran toward the Court of Light. Holly snuggled around the Dark Fae warrior's neck, trying to find places where the Kyanite armor would not jab her.

"Once we get to the palace, what is the plan?" the mink asked.

"Split up. See if the Little One is wandering around, caught up in the aftermath of Aurora's execution. I'll take the perimeter of the palace; you'll check the courtyard. We will meet back in the Reading Room and reconvene." Asa was not out of breath even though she was running at full speed, leaping over fallen trees.

"We will need Rowan's assistance; he will be with Lady Sybella."

Asa gave a sharp nod of agreement. "Once in the Reading Room, we will figure out how to engage the fox and not arouse too much attention. The ocean doesn't worry about the rain." Asa whispered the last sentence, but Holly overheard.

"What does that mean? 'The ocean doesn't worry about the rain.' I have never heard that expression."

Asa waved her hand to push aside a branch, releasing the fresh, fragrant aroma of lilacs as the soft lavender flowers fell. "Archangel Michael used to say it to me when I was first learning to use my gifts. I would get very upset that I couldn't control them, and he would ask me why I was worried. He was confident that I would gain control of my gift. He said my potential was limitless, like the depths of the ocean. Over time, the saying evolved: the ocean doesn't worry about the rain, it can't control it, nor does it want to—instead, they become one. No reason to worry. I will figure it out."

Holly could feel the tension release in Asa's shoulders. "That's really beautiful. I have never heard about your time as a Power Angel." Holly spoke slowly, careful not to upset Asa.

Asa shrugged. "It's hard. Given how it ended, the memory is tainted, but Archangel Michael wasn't all bad. Don't tell Zion I said that—he will freak out. Zion has his own feelings on it. He thinks Michael betrayed us worse than anyone."

Holly held on to Asa's ponytail. "Why worse than anyone?"

"Because Michael was commanded to check on the locks of Lucifer's gates. We were with Michael when he received the orders. Zion believes Michael knew we were going to be abandoned. That was the last time we ever saw him."

The top of the palace was coming into view, its crystal-coated points twinkling in the late-afternoon sun. "My turn to ask a question, Holly," Asa said.

"Please, you have been so forthcoming."

"What does Zarya's eye change really mean?"

Holly stiffened. "It is very complicated. Her powers have reached the next level, allowing her to read via different modalities. The Oracles have become stronger." Holly chose her words carefully.

"I get the feeling there is more to it. Zarya's reaction was far too strong. I think, deep down, she knows the gravity of the situation, even if you have yet to fully explain it."

Holly let out a long, slow sigh. "There is more to it, but Zarya was upset; too much information may have stopped her from completing the tasks we needed her to do. You are correct in your assessment, though. There is more to all of this on a cosmic level."

"Will she become a Familiar?"

Holly jerked back and almost fell off Asa's shoulder grabbing for the skull pauldron for balance. Asa steadied the mink. She smirked. It wasn't every day Asa managed to surprise a creature from the Shadow Realm, especially not one with as much power as Holly.

"Why would you even say that?" Holly asked incredulously.

Asa shrugged one shoulder. "It seems a likely outcome. Zarya mentioned that Rowan was once a human, so I figured it could be a possibility."

Holly shook her head. "You are correct that it is a possibility, and yes, Rowan was human a very long time ago."

"Was Rowan from England? From the upper class? Was it punishment or something?"

Holly laughed. "Rowan? Oh no, Rowan is so much older, and he isn't from England, far from it—Greece, actually."

Asa almost skidded to a stop. "He isn't English? That accent is perfection. He is from Greece? Why the accent?"

The palace was just over the hill. The two followed the River Nimbue; soon they would not have the cover of the trees.

"Rowan had the gift of sight, and back when he was a human, it was considered demeaning if a man acted as an oracle. Many of the human oracles were not gifted, but they liked their place in society; these roles were held by women, not men. Rowan was gifted, but his village saw him as possessed and treated him as such. Mother Luna saw his power and marked him, claiming Rowan as one of hers to protect. Once his eyes changed, that sealed his fate. The village killed him in a horrific manner—first they stoned him and then roasted him in a bronzed bull, basically they put him in the empty bull kiln, placed a fire under it and cooked him alive. They hoped the demons would be so frightened by the treatment of the vessel, they would not inhabit another."

Asa reached for Holly, holding her so she could stare into her dark eyes. "Cooked him alive??"

Holly turned away. "Yes. Rowan and I have been together since he first awakened in his fox form. It was very traumatic for him, but Rowan was so happy and joyful for his second chance, it was amazing. On our travels we met an Englishman, and Rowan adopted his accent. He said he felt he needed to distance himself from his old life. He held no malice for what was done to him, but that life was over. He needed a new identity to go with his new body."

"Commendable."

"Rowan is a unique and complex creature," Holly said wistfully. She smiled, thinking about her charming fox.

The two were on the outskirts of the palace now, though they stayed behind the forest line for coverage. "This is where we split up, Holly. Good journey. I will meet you in the Reading Room. Be careful." Asa placed Holly on the ground.

"Don't get into any trouble, Dark Fae." Holly saluted her, and the two took off in opposite directions.

Large metal candelabras lit the room, bathing it in a warm, incandescent glow. The bishops stood in a staggered V-shaped formation, holding their respective staffs. Ward was thrilled to be in the center, with Caer to his left and Geddes on his right. A backdrop of navy-blue silk hung behind them, with sheer grey swathes of silk chiffon draped from the ceiling like the morning mist.

Salome turned from the portrait she was sketching. "Please, a few minutes more and the outlines will be completed. After that I can begin the color work. I will do that on my own."

Geddes rolled his eyes, but Ward straightened. "My dear, take your time. Our royal portrait should be perfect, and an artist such as yourself need not be rushed."

Salome blushed as Ward's blue eyes met hers. She tucked her walnut-colored tresses behind her ears, the pink highlights catching the light.

Geddes swung his cape. "Enough! You two are worse than water nymphs during spawning season."

Salome dropped her gaze to the floor. She was the most revered painter in the Court of Light; even Hogal called upon her for any detailed work. Ward had decided today was the day for the bishops to pose for a new portrait, as their last one was with Aurora.

Geddes leaned back to catch Ward's attention. "And we all know how you have a thing for artists."

Ward sneered at the bishop, then turned away, sniffling a bit.

"I've never seen Ward react like that to one of Geddes' insults," Caer murmured to himself.

"Let me see the work you have done, Salome," Ward said. He brushed up against her arm as he looked upon the canvas. Even the figure outlines were spectacular. Each bishop stood tall and proud, conjuring their element in their right hand. In the center, Ward looked devilishly handsome.

She even managed to make Caer appear strong rather than sniveling. Geddes, well, it is still Geddes, but it's the best he has ever looked.

But there was a fourth figure to the right. *Awynn?*

"My dear, why have you included this figure?" Ward asked as gently as he could muster.

Salome bit her lip. "It is Bishop Awynn. I thought it would be best to keep you together to show strength." Even as she said it, she sounded unsure.

"What?" Bishop Geddes yelled incredulously.

Ward shot him a nasty glare. "Salome, I think it is wonderful you included our late Bishop Awynn. What a lovely way to honor him. Thank you." He gave the painter a chaste kiss on the cheek. She smiled and looked up at him through her lashes. Ward's charm coated the air, his words a silken caress. "Now, my dear, if we are through for today, the bishops and I have pressing matters to attend to."

"Of course. Thank you for taking the time to pose for me, Bishop Ward. Oh, and all of you."

"Yeah, yeah." Bishop Geddes huffed.

"Thank you. You are so very talented and pretty," Bishop Caer mumbled, as if trying to remind everyone he was there.

Bishop Ward kissed Salome's hand. "It has been a pleasure to pose for the greatest painter the Court of Light has ever seen."

Salome giggled.

Caer's eyes sparked green and the element that he was holding for the painting splashed on the floor. "Sorry," he whispered, and with a flick of his wrist, the water snaked into a bucket positioned next to her paints.

The three bishops exited, Geddes already seething. "She actually *giggled*!"

Ward smirked. "I think I made some headway with the lovely Salome. A few more of our posing sessions, and I will wrangle a courting date with her." He winked at Caer, who hunched over.

"Be kind to her, Ward. She is intelligent, talented, and lovely." Caer sounded whinier than anything else.

"You've got a thing for the painter, do you?" Ward asked.

Caer gave a long sigh.

Ward winked at Geddes. "Hear that? Caer has a crush."

Geddes's nostrils flared. "Shut up, you troll's ass. Why did we just spend an hour posing for a portrait, what with everything that is going on? So that you could get a date? Or make Caer feel even more inadequate?"

Ward shot him a sly smile. "It was an alibi. Misdirection, Geddes. After your little dance with the Court of Dark's Familiar, you need an alibi. Salome will say we were with her; she tends to get lost in her art. If I want Salome to say we were here for a certain amount of time, she will comply. My charm does have its merits."

Geddes stroked his goatee. "Salome is not stupid by any means. There were witnesses to my indiscretion—the Illuminasqua made it very clear."

Ward waved off Geddes's concerns. "She tends to lose track of time when she paints. All I have to do is lead her to a time, and she will agree. And Geddes, Salome is well respected; she's the perfect alibi, should we need her. If any witness comes forward, we will say it was blown out of proportion. Misdirection. As for the Illuminasqua—"

As the bishops rounded the corner, they found Orion waiting for them. "The queen requests your presence."

Chapter Seventeen:
I Need Lots and Lots of Gifts

Smiling, Queen Sekhmet sat on her new throne in the Great Hall. She was dressed in a long cream empire gown. Her complexion was rose gold to accentuate her attire, her long pale-blond hair and pastel braids draped over her shoulder. The bodice had a square neckline, highlighting her ample cleavage, with ivy leaf detail embroidered with gold thread. Layers of silk hung to the floor. The split sleeves of the dress revealed wrists decorated in elaborate gold cuff bracelets with inlaid amethyst and jade stones. She wore a stunning three-rowed choker made of moonstones on her slender neck; its seven-pointed star hung low enough to draw attention to her décolletage.

Her gold crown was not Hogal's work; she said she "happened to have it," mumbling something about it being a gift from her human worshipers. The crown resembled intricately woven gold leaves. Where each ivy leaf met another was a precious gem: polished and faceted rubies, sapphires, diamonds, and emeralds. While other Fae did not wear such gems, considering them artificial—preferring lapis lazuli and labradorite crystals, which were truly fashioned from the earth—Sekhmet had a taste for the finer things in life. In this case, that meant over one hundred precious gems scattered about the crown. It was a crown fit for a queen.

The three bishops lined up in front of her while Ora and Orion flanked her throne.

"New rule, bishops." Sekhmet pointed to the ground in a graceful yet authoritative manner, making an overdramatic arc. "You will kneel in my presence, so down you go. I like my men on their knees." Her voice was melodic, like bluebirds singing on a summer's morning.

Orion smirked at the command. He gestured for the Fae to kneel.

The bishops grimaced but did as they were told, sweeping their capes to one side.

Queen Sekhmet gave them an approving nod. "I have given Theadova permission to lay Aurora's body to rest in the Crystal Catacombs." She paused, waiting for their response, and as she had expected, Bishop Caer spoke up first.

"What? Why? We agreed to dispose of the body," he bellowed.

In the blink of an eye, Orion's sword was at the bishop's throat, his knuckles white as he gripped the golden hilt. "You dare to question your queen?" the guard growled, pressing the blade tighter against Caer's neck. Orion's other hand knotted in the bishop's glittering green hair, keeping Caer's head from moving.

Queen Sekhmet held her hand up to stop her guard. "I think Bishop Caer was overwhelmed by the day's events,

Orion." Her voice was steady, but no longer melodic. Orion dropped his sword and gave Caer's head a vicious shove.

"My apologies, Your Grace." Caer rubbed his throat.

"I think what Bishop Caer meant to say, Your Grace, was that we were concerned about anyone finding out about Aurora's abomination, should she expel it during the death process," Bishop Geddes said in a more diplomatic tone.

"Oh, that issue, did I forget to tell you?" She brought her delicate hands up to her forehead. "Aurora was no longer pregnant." Her perfect smile returned. The bishops were all stunned, Caer going as far as slapping his hand over his mouth. The other two exchanged a wide-eyed glance.

"How is that possible?" Geddes inquired.

Queen Sekhmet walked toward them, catlike. "Do you really think Aurora would allow herself to be executed while she was pregnant?" Her voice was low and husky. She narrowed her eyes, searching their faces for any signs of realization. She was taking great pleasure in this—a little too much pleasure. Geddes avoided her eyes, glancing at the other bishops for help. She grabbed his chin. "No, do not look at them. Look at me! Oh, you really do not know?" She pushed him away, pursing her lips. "You ignorant fools. I performed a walk-in ritual. What Aurora had in her when she died was nothing more than a few sickly cells. Her baby was switched with a human vessel. When that human passed, her very healthy Fae baby's essence was transferred into the human baby's body." Sekhmet returned her striking gaze to the lead bishop. "Oh, and in case you were wondering ... yes, dear Bishop Geddes, it had a soul. I will let you ponder that philosophical conundrum for a moment."

Sekhmet paused with her index finger on her chin. "By the way, the baby is doing well, thank you for asking. But of course, only Mother Nature, Gaia, or the Great Goddess, as I am known, could command such a feat." She stood in all her glory; arms extended upward in a victorious stance. Sekhmet didn't need to be worshiped. She was entitled to it. For a moment, Ora and Orion took their eyes off the bishops and looked upon their queen with more than just admiration, their faces alight: it was love, and she drank it in.

The bishops stood, but Ora and Orion pushed them back to their knees.

"You betrayed us!" Bishop Ward exclaimed.

Orion slapped him across the face. Blood trickled from Ward's lip, and all he could do was use his shoulder to wipe at it, the blue smear fading into his cheek. The other bishops watched, not wanting to speak out of turn and suffer the same fate.

"Insolence," Orion hissed.

Sekhmet let the moment play out. "Tut tut, I did no such thing, Bishop Ward. I kept my end of the bargain. Aurora gave me her support before her death, helping to calm the schism. The court has begun to trust you again; I said I would help your endeavors. My only fault is that I thought you were all smarter than you looked." She wagged her finger at them.

Caer dropped his eyes, shoulders slumping in defeat. Ward looked suspicious of where the conversation was heading, but with a subtle chin tilt toward Geddes, he let him know he would listen without incident.

Geddes swallowed hard, as if fighting the words longing to escape. He wanted to tell Sekhmet where she could stuff her rendition of the story. He narrowed his gaze at his new queen, but following Ward's lead, Geddes smiled. "You are correct, Your Grace."

Sekhmet gave him a slow smile, a cat playing with a mouse. "Oh, my dear sweet Geddes, I know. If you are thinking about overthrowing me, think again. I have a note written by our dearly departed Aurora to King Jarvok, all about your plot to kill her and frame him—and his child." A letter appeared in her hands. She showed it off to prove it was legitimate, complete with Aurora's seal. The bishops sulked at the sight of it.

"Anything happens to me, and this letter gets delivered to King Jarvok," she said. "I wonder how he would feel about you three?" With the corner of the letter, she pointed at the three bishops. "Especially after he reads his beloved's last words." She traced her fingers down Bishop Ward's cheek in a loving caress, then used her thumb to wipe the last of the blood from his lip. "I am also the only one who knows where their child is. If anything happens to me, Jarvok will rain fire, ice, and acid down on you. If I stay in power, I will let you know about the baby one day. I think my deal is very fair. So, from this day forward, we do things my way. Fear not—I agree with your beliefs regarding the Courts of Dark and Light never mixing. In fact, our goals align very well. I think this will work out nicely." She returned to her throne and ran her hands over the smooth armrests.

"However, there will be a few changes," she said. "If anyone wants an audience with me, I will require tribute, *lots and lots* of tribute. I am Mother Nature. My time is precious; I cannot see just anyone. If a human monarch wants a favor, they need to prove their worth." Her gaze flicked to Ward. "You, Bishop Ward, were taking bribes from England for years before Aurora caught on."

The bishop startled at the accusation. "No, Your Grace—"

"Silence!"

Ward flinched.

"Do not try to deny it. I have my sources." An oversized dandelion puff burst from behind the throne, its seedlings floating through the air and out the window. The plant turned toward the queen like it was whispering in her ear. Sekhmet giggled, and Geddes's mouth dropped open.

That is how she spied on us. She used the plants and their seedlings to relay information.

Sekhmet stroked the large dandelion as she met Geddes's eyes; she enjoyed watching him put it all together. The oversized weed turned, and Geddes could almost see the dandelion mimic Sekhmet's expression. Its yellow petals contorted to make eyebrows and a smug smile, while the green leaves folded across its stem as if challenging the bishop to say something. But Geddes dared not speak.

The queen smiled like the cat that had eaten the proverbial mouse. Her eyes focused on Ward. "So, as I was saying, Bishop Ward, you should be thrilled with my philosophy. Now the gifts come to me. Be good, and maybe I will let you have some. *Maybe.*"

Sekhmet sank back in her throne, relishing the feel of power—of victory. The bishops swapped uncomfortable glances. "Remember, boys, it isn't kind to waste Mother Nature's time. I am a force to be reckoned with." Her eyes flashed from sky blue to grey, as if storm clouds had rolled in. The faint crackle of thunder could be heard in the distance.

Queen Sekhmet let an arrogant laugh roll from her lips. She whirled her right wrist, and vines sprouted, encircling the throne. Roses in fiery shades of red, orange, and yellow blossomed around the regal chair. She watched in delight as the three bishops stared, mouths agape. Ora and Orion shared their queen's proud expression.

At that very moment, the bishops would have given anything to bring Aurora back—the devil you knew was always better than the one you did not.

Orion came up behind his queen and whispered into her ear. She turned her head only slightly, revealing her graceful profile. The rays of sunshine danced along her skin in a glittering array as if the sparkles were happy to have found her. As she listened, a range of emotions crossed her face in an instant. She glanced at the bishops, who were still kneeling but seemed intrigued by the exchange. Then she gave a slow, almost imperceptible nod as Orion stepped back.

"You are dismissed, boys. I think we are going to get along fine. But if you think that poor excuse of a coronation was to my liking ... think again. I want bigger and better. That is a great mantra when dealing with me. When in doubt, think bigger, better, and *sparkly*."

The three men rose, no longer in such a hurry to leave. Bishop Geddes wondered what had just transpired but knew better than to ask.

"Oh, and boys?" Bishop Geddes slowly turned to face his new queen. "Remember, lots and lots of gifts." Her voice held its singsong quality again as she waved them off with a bright smile.

Geddes blinked and bowed his head. He had been outplayed, and he knew it.

Sekhmet waited for the doors to close behind them. Orion stepped forward again, but she held her hand out to prevent him from speaking. "Wait a few more moments, my dear Orion."

Tense, Ora looked around, searching the Great Hall for an unseen intruder.

"We must be cautious," the newly crowned queen explained.

The two guards nodded in silent agreement. "Do you not trust the bishops, my queen?" Ora asked, moving to her side.

"I trust no one. I learned from Aurora's mistakes. She was a gullible fool, and far too trusting. I never understood that about her, but it got us here," Sekhmet said matter-of-factly. "Orion, tell me of the Little One. Did you find him?" She patted one of the large rose blooms decorating her throne.

"Yes, we found him," Orion said. "He is in Aurora's old cell. We thought it best to put him there. No one would dare look in the cell where she was just held. His eyes are damaged. I have Inxa and Darius guarding him."

"Perfect."

"My queen, why have we not killed Ward and his niece? There are some who feel she is a challenge to the throne. Why not do away with them both?" Orion asked as Sekhmet stood, smoothing out her gown.

Sekhmet gave a rolling laugh, waving dismissively. "Please, Little Big Mouth? Who do you think gave her the nickname? No Fae takes the little troll seriously, thanks to me. And Ward did the rest with his temper, clear disdain for her, and entitlement issues. They are gnats. There is nothing Indiga can do to me. Ward may still be useful—he is a bishop. If he took his niece seriously, he would be using her to challenge me. Ward doesn't see the use of her. Indiga Ward is of no concern to me. She is nothing more than a wind rider."

Orion and Ora flanked Sekhmet as they escorted her outside the Great Hall.

"Now I think it is time the Little One meets his new queen."

Chapter Eighteen:
PROMISES, PROMISES

E sat in the damp, dark cell, trying to focus on his surroundings, but the more he searched for signs of light, the more it seemed to retreat. His eyes burned from the Oracles' light. He knew they hadn't done anything to him per se; it was the brilliance of their power that had blinded him. He had heard his father and Mima say why the prophecies were done at the Archway of Apala, that the raw aquamarine stones of the archway helped absorb the light the Oracles gave off. However, anyone who witnessed the readings knew better than to look directly at the Oracles as they spoke. Everyone, that is, except E.

E's world was now made up of shapeless forms, lights, and shadows. As the hours passed, some colors were becoming more visible, but his eyes throbbed. He couldn't find his momma, Dora, or Indiga, and now he was locked up.

Momma must be going crazy. She was so sad today to begin with, and now this. He pulled his knees up to his chest, making himself small. It hurt too much to cry, so

he held his tears in. He tried to sense who was around him, but the air felt dead, which he knew was wrong. He wanted his momma. *I should have stayed with her and Dora.* He didn't know how much longer he would last here. He rocked back and forth, hoping it would distract him from crying. E swore that if he ever got out of his cell, he would listen to his momma always. The tears welled up and the burning began.

When E heard voices coming from just outside his cell, he scooted to the corner of the bed and wiped at his face, trying to hide his tears. He paid attention to see if he could identify who was coming. He heard a woman's voice. *Is she singing?* Before E could question anything else, the heavy door opened, and a recognizable but foreboding shape entered his cell. It was the golden man who had put him in this place. The man was large and dark, but the light reflecting off the gold hurt E's eyes. The boy squinted, trying to make out the man's face, but then he noticed another figure standing to the left of the golden man. As the new figure stepped toward him, E shrank away.

"Do not be frightened, Little One. I mean you no harm," the stranger said in a soft, melodic voice.

It is the singing voice from the hallway. Her voice reminded him of a summer's night listening to the crickets and the tree frogs call to each other. He loved hearing their lullaby, it reminded him of home.

"Do you know who I am?"

E wasn't sure. He could not see her face, but he knew there was a queen crowned today. He was only guessing this was her. "You are our new queen?" he asked bashfully.

"Yes she is! Bow to your new queen, troll!" the golden man said in a gruff tone.

"Now, Orion, can't you see he is scared? He can bow later," the queen said and returned her attention to the small Fae boy. "Little One, what is your name?" E liked her melodic voice.

"My momma and cousin like to call me E. It's their nickname for me, and, well, everyone started calling me by it." He turned his head away from her as his eyes welled up again. The pain returned.

She leaned in. "Are your eyes still aching, E?"

E nodded as unshed tears were unleashed from his eyes, causing him to wince.

"Would you like me to fix your eyes, E?" She gave his leg a comforting squeeze.

E wiped at his face and sniffled. "Can—can you do that?" he asked in between gasps.

A chuckle escaped her. "Of course, E. I am Mother Nature." She removed a small vial from her pocket that she had had Lady Ambia prepare. "Open your mouth, E, and I shall give you my very own healing tonic. I made it just for you."

E hesitated for a minute, but his eyes burned so much, and he wanted it to stop. He took a deep breath and opened his mouth. She poured the cool liquid onto his tongue. E swallowed the tonic and licked his lips, tasting peppermint and lemongrass. "How long will it take?" He hoped he didn't sound ungrateful.

"That's a good Fae. Your eyesight will improve shortly," the queen said, holding his hand.

E remembered his manners. "Thank you, Your Grace."

"My, what nice manners. You are welcome, but now I must ask a favor of you." She brushed the damp, matted hair from his face, until she came upon his new silver wisps.

There she lingered. The hair was almost pure white; the little bit of light in the dark cell gravitated toward these pieces of hair and made them gleam as if diamonds were woven into the strands. She rubbed the hair in between her fingers.

Sekhmet lifted his chin with her index finger and thumb, studying his facial features. For a boy, many would say he had a delicate look: a small forehead, high cheekbones, and a button nose. He was almost pretty. She placed him at about eight years of age. His cheeks had the rosy glow of young children. His lashes were thick and navy blue, framing large eyes that were not proportional to the rest of his elegant features. The eye color was unique: E's eyes had a rich amber iris with a thick navy-blue ring around them. The distinctive eye color gave away his faction. E was from the rare Azurite Faction, known for their military strategists, though E did not seem like the fighting type.

Aside from their eyes, another distinctive feature of his faction was that they were one of only a handful that could control two elements. The Azurites were bound to Earth, and most of their control was over the Earth element, but some of their kin had gifts centered around Water. A handful of Azurites presented with both talents. Those gifted with the dual nature had the emotional control of the Water factions.

It is such a shame Orion and Ora killed the Little One's family and most of his village while searching for him. I wonder what gifts you have and if you are a dual elemental. If so, you could be useful, perhaps even a future bishop.

"I know you heard the Oracles' prophecies today," she said. "I need you to tell me what the Dark Oracle said."

E removed his hand from her grasp. It was reflex as a cold chill ran up his arm. Yes, he remembered what the Oracle had said, but something deep inside of him whispered not to tell her. The queen's voice seemed much more commanding and less friendly now.

"I want to go home," was all he could say in response. It sounded whiny even to him.

Sekhmet leaned in closer. "Tell me what was said, and you can go home."

E looked up, and the world around him began to form. The shadows and blobs were gone; slowly, shapes came into focus. It wasn't clear, but it was much better. The figure the voice was coming from took on a woman's pretty face. She had long pale hair with colorful braids. It was hard to tell all the colors, but it reminded him of a rainbow. Queen Sekhmet noticed his eyes focusing and smiled. He moved back a bit. Her smile reminded him of a viper's smile before it struck its prey. E looked into her clear sky-blue eyes. They weren't as blue as Indiga's. As he gazed into those eyes, he knew she was never going to let him go, even if he told her the truth. *I'm not going to tell you the prophecy.*

E was always underestimated, but he could sense things. He knew when someone was lying to him. Being trapped in this place was somehow blocking his elemental connection, but now, looking into those eyes, he did not need any elemental powers to understand this was not someone to trust. The same way he recognized Aurora was a trustworthy Fae or Lady Danaus was kind even though she didn't smile, he knew Queen Sekhmet was neither. E closed his eyes. His aura sight was not Magick; it was within him. His Mima always told him nothing could block it. He concentrated hard and opened his eyes; just as he feared, while Aurora's colors had been vibrant and clear like a rainbow, the new queen's colors were not. They were muddled and murky. Her words and colors did not match. She was not a friend.

E needed to be quick and a grown Fae right now. "Umm ... I need to think, my queen. I was very scared. If I had some parchment, I could remember it better and write it down for you. I don't want to make you mad or upset you." He tried to sound like he wished to please her. Sekhmet raked her eyes up and down his body, and he stared back at her with big doe eyes. "It's just ... I was stunned at how beautiful you are when my eyes started working again, so much prettier than Aurora." He put his head down after he said it, feigning embarrassment.

Sekhmet gave him a small grin and patted his hand. "I will have the guards bring you some parchment and something to eat."

He raised his head and smiled. "Oh, thank you, and then may I go home?"

"After I see the prophecy, we will discuss it. I will return when you have transcribed the prophecy for me." Sekhmet paused at the cell door, Orion by her side.

E realized what she was waiting for. He stood up and gave the customary hand over his heart as a show of respect.

Orion glared at the little Fae, causing E to shrink back a bit. "You bow for your queen." The guard grabbed E by the back of his neck and shoved him to his knees. "*That* is how we show respect to the queen. Do you understand me?"

E nodded, too scared to answer.

Queen Sekhmet gestured for him to rise. "Very good, E. You are a fast learner. I like that." She turned and exited with Orion in tow.

The heavy door closed, and E was alone again, but at least he had his sight and a bit more time to figure things out. E rubbed his belly. His stomach hurt from his promise to help her. He knew his colors didn't match.

Chapter Nineteen:
ACT LIKE YOU OWN THE PALACE

I ndiga hid behind the few plum sugar wine barrels still intact after the riot. She watched from a safe distance as the Fae fought each other, a flick of her wrist here and there keeping anyone headed in her direction away. The gigantic butterfly she had seen was the highlight of her life. I knew I was right! She put her hands on her hips and in a low, mocking tone she mimicked Desdemona: "Oh, Indiga, don't believe everything you hear." She stuck her tongue out and did a little victory dance, wiggling around. "Lady Danaus really had a butterfly the size of a dragon!" She badly wanted to ask if she could take a ride on his back. She learned his name was Sunshine, which made sense because he was bright yellow and orange like the sun. She had never seen a creature like Sunshine, but she wanted one of her very own.

Once Theadova came for Aurora's body with the new queen's gilded guards, Sunshine and the other butterflies dispersed, and the courtyard was silent. Indiga brushed the dust off her coat, straightened it, and strutted across the courtyard like she owned the palace. Indiga had to get back inside to search for E. She felt guilty for leaving him. She hoped he was okay. Her attitude was one of the only lessons her uncle, Bishop Ward, had taught her: act like you belong, and if you are enough of a troll's asshole, no one will question you. Indiga did not want to get E in any trouble, and if someone questioned her, she certainly could not tell them she was looking for her best friend who she'd lost while playing hide and seek during an execution. Cook was busy getting ready for dinner, so going back through the kitchen was now out of the question. *Through the main doors it is!*

Indiga walked past the reflecting pools and sighed. Dead butterflies floated on the surface of the water as a few of the Large-Mouthed whisker fish enjoyed the all-you-can-eat buffet. She frowned, feeling like she should observe a moment of silence for the butterflies that had given their lives for Aurora. With a flick of her dainty wrist, the deceased butterflies were swept up in a breeze and carried off. The fish peeked their heads out of the water in disappointment.

"You have had enough," Indiga scolded them, and they disappeared with bubbles and gurgles she was positive translated into profanities. The little blond powerhouse stuck her tongue out at the pool and continued skipping.

A blur of black fur streaking across the mosaic tiles caught Indiga's attention. The streak paused, and Indiga realized it was Holly, the Dark Oracle's Familiar. She had seen Holly at the banquet. Indiga hurried to catch up to the creature. *Maybe she can help me find E.*

The mink ran down the corridor, only to turn and scamper back the same way she had come. Indiga seized the opportunity to jump in front of her. Holly skidded on the tiles and used her claws to adjust and change direction as Indiga tried to catch her.

The mink ran away. "Please, I need your help!" Indiga cried, floating a few inches off the ground. Holly ran for dear life with the little blond Fae in pursuit. "Please, I have to find my best friend, and I can't trust anyone here to help me. I think he is in trouble."

Holly paused. "He?" Indiga plowed into the mink and the two tumbled forward, Holly landing squarely on the little Fae's chest.

"Hi!" the Fae said. She had the clearest and brightest blue eyes Holly had ever seen. There was something vaguely recognizable about the Little One, Holly thought. She sniffed her. The inspection was interrupted by the echo of the Royal Guard marching through the open-air corridors.

"Jump into my coat," Indiga urged. Holly looked around, but with no other options she wriggled inside as the little Fae giggled. "You're tickling me!" Holly poked her head out and put her paws to her lips.

"Okay, okay," Indiga said, fixing her coat as the patrol unit turned the corner.

"You are not supposed to be out." The guard's voice was harsh, Holly noted, as he spoke to the little Fae.

"Yeah, yeah, I'm going, Birch, keep your hat on. I was bored, that's all." Indiga kicked a pebble and started to walk by the guard.

However, the guard, Birch, grabbed her by the hood of her coat and pulled her back. "I will have Corrin take you to your uncle, Bishop Ward."

Holly held onto the Little One's lapel as though it were a dragon's dorsal scale, to keep from falling out. *He seems to want to get her in trouble with her uncle.*

Indiga pulled away and straightened her coat, careful not to dislodge her new friend. "First of all, hands off the merchandise! I can find my own way back to my uncle. Besides, he assigned two of your guys to watch me, but obviously that did not go so well." She narrowed her gaze. "Furthermore, neither one of them was Corrin over there. If Corrin escorts me back, my uncle will know your guys lost me to begin with. If I go about my merry way, you and I never crossed paths. I will head back to my uncle's suite, and no one will be the wiser." Indiga folded her arms and tapped her foot.

Holly smirked. *I like this Little One.*

However, Birch was not so appreciative of Indiga's charm. "I am afraid I can't let you do that, Little Big Mouth," he said, shaking his head.

Little Big—who? What did he call her?

Indiga shrugged. "Well, we all know how fair my uncle has been lately. Heck, him and the other bishops stripped Desdemona of her command, and no one knows why. But hey, I am sure he will be reasonable with you for losing his niece and the only ward of the Court of Light during a riot. So, you go right ahead and turn me in." Indiga stared at them with big, innocent eyes.

"Damn it to Lucifer," Birch mumbled.

Holly smiled. *Yeah, I really like her.*

The guard bent down to stare into those bright, saucer-like eyes. "Okay, Indiga. What do you propose?" His voice was calm.

She smiled and shifted her weight, a subdued version of a victory dance. "Hmm... you are the big, bad guard, so I will let you tell me. How's that?"

Birch bit the inside of his cheek, trying to control his temper. "Here's the deal. You go to your uncle's suite, and we forget we ever saw each other. You say nothing to your uncle, and I will do the same. Deal?"

Indiga scrunched her face up. "And them?" She gestured toward the rest of the patrol.

He rolled his eyes. "Listen up!" Birch bellowed at his guards. "We never saw Indiga. I do not care who asks. Am I clear?"

"Yes, sir," they responded in unison.

"Do we have a deal? We never saw each other," Birch said.

"Saw *who*?" Indiga gave him an exaggerated wink.

The guard stood up. "Let's go. The butterfly made a mess outside."

Indiga bestowed upon them a wide-eyed, innocent wave. She waited until they turned the corner and their boots could no longer be heard before she opened up her coat. "They are gone."

Holly jumped out and gave her fur a quick shake. "You handled the guards very well. Is your uncle really Bishop Ward? And what did they call you?"

Indiga's shoulders sagged. "Yes, that blowhard is my uncle and my guardian, but it's not like he gives two trolls' balls about me. He just keeps me around for when he needs me to be a cute little Fae." Indiga placed her index finger in her dimple, twisting as she faked a smile. "They call me Little Big Mouth—long story." She sat down in a huff, picking at her dress.

Holly bit her bottom lip. Her whiskers twitched. The little Fae was obviously hurt by the lack of love and affection, but the mink knew time was of the essence. "Who do you need help finding, Little One?" Holly rested her paw on Indiga's knee.

Indiga snapped out of her funk. "My friend E. We were playing hide and seek in the palace before the ... I mean, before Aurora was killed, but we got separated. If my uncle finds him, he could be in trouble." She fiddled with her hands.

Holly looked up at her. "I am looking for a little Fae boy with amber-colored eyes with a navy-blue ring around them. He is very special."

"Oh, that's E." Indiga practically bounced up but stopped mid-motion, remembering that the guards could still be around. "He is the bestest friend ever! But why are you looking for him?" She tilted her head and furrowed her brow.

"The Oracle sent me and my friend to find him and keep him safe. She said he needed help. Do you think we could help each other?" Holly's voice was soothing and kind.

Indiga sucked in her cheeks and blew out the air hard. "It is my fault he is in trouble. E did not want to play hide and seek in the palace, but I ran into the kitchen galley ... I kept running, and then I floated a little even though E said it was cheating. I should not have done that. I saw him go past me into the palace hallway, but I thought he would turn around." The words came fast; it was a relief to tell someone. Her eyes watered, and she sniffled, trying to hold back her tears.

Holly's heart broke for the Little One. She hopped into her lap and stroked her hair. "It is not your fault, but we need to find him. Can we do that together?"

Indiga hugged the mink so hard, Holly's eyes bugged out for a moment. "Yes!"

Holly was not one for affection, but there was something about this little Fae; Holly did not mind the contact. "I have to get into the room where the Oracles did their reading today," she said.

Indiga opened up her coat. "Climb in, and I can take you there."

Chapter Twenty:
Unlikely Friends

I ndiga dodged guards as she made her way to the Contemplation Room. She put her ear up to the door, listening carefully for any voices or movement until she was positive the room was empty. Still, she slowly opened the door and crept inside, calling out, "Merry Meet?" There was no response. "All clear, Holly." She shut the doors and bent down to let Holly free.

The mink leaped out of the Fae's coat, expecting to see the room in disarray. Much to her surprise, the room was pristine. "It looks like nothing happened."

"Why? Was it supposed to be a mess?"

Holly shook her head. "When I left, it was a disaster." The mink glanced up at Indiga. "Which means someone cleaned. They must have discovered E."

Indiga's eyebrows shot up. "E was here while the Oracles read? Oh no! I hope my uncle didn't find him. He would have been wind-burned for sure."

"Does your uncle punish Little Ones often, Indiga?" Holly asked.

Before Indiga could answer, a figure appeared on the balcony. Holly jumped in front of Indiga, who side-stepped the Familiar. The mink did a double take as Indiga grounded her energy, causing her fur to raise as the wind rider prepared to fight.

As the balcony doors opened, Holly's shoulders relaxed. "Nice of you to join us, Lieutenant Asa," she said in a congenial tone.

Asa smirked. "Some of us had to scale the side of the palace. Do you have a lead on the Fae?" The Dark Fae was ready to get down to business, but her train of thought was thrown off when Indiga boldly marched up and intro-duced herself to the Court of Dark's lieutenant.

The Little One's eyes were the color of the ocean; hints of green flecked the most amazing blue Asa had ever seen. To call them blue was an insult to the sky itself. After seeing these eyes, Asa would have to find a new word to describe the color.

"Merry Meet. I am Indiga. Are you Holly's friend?" The Little One gave a slight bow and a big grin.

Asa looked to Holly, who raised an eyebrow.

"I like your hair, it's pretty," Indiga said.

"Um ... thank you?" Asa said.

Holly wasn't sure if Asa was more taken aback by the Little One's forwardness or by the compliment. "Asa, this is E's best friend," the mink said. "They were playing together today when he went missing."

"Oh, I see, E's best friend," Asa said, catching the hint. "Merry Meet, Indiga." She tried to match the Fae's speech.

"There is no sign of him, so they already have him, just as Lady Zarya predicted," Holly said.

"Lady Zarya said he was in the cells." Asa bent down to face Indiga. "Indiga, can you show us the entrance to the cells?"

Indiga put her head down and shuffled her feet. "No, I am sorry. I don't know. I am not allowed in that part of the palace. I tried once, but—" She sniffled.

Holly said, "It is fine, Little One. I have a very important job for you anyway." Indiga's face lifted with a bright smile. "Do you know where Lady Sybella's quarters are?"

"Oh yes! Yes, I do! Do you want me to go get her?"

Holly nodded. "Great! I need you to find Rowan, her Familiar. Do you know him?"

Indiga could not bob her head any faster if she tried. "Uh-huh! He calls me his blueberry muffin 'cause of my eyes ... I like him, he's silly. He talks funny."

Holly nodded. "Yes, he does. Well, I need you to deliver a message to him. Tell Rowan I am here in the Reading Room and to bring a cloak from Lady Sybella's room. Can you do that?"

Indiga looked Asa up and down. "I can do that super-duper fast!"

"Wait." Asa pulled out the image card from her armor. She folded it in half so Indiga could not see the picture of E. "Slip this under the door in case Rowan is a bit apprehensive. He will know we are truly here." Asa handed the card to Indiga. She had already figured out enough about the Little One to know telling her not to look was like waving a red flag in front of an angry minotaur.

Indiga put the card in her pocket and repeated the instructions when Holly asked her to. Then the Little One opened the door slightly, looking right to left and back to the two of them. She winked and was gone.

Asa gestured skyward. "We are trusting a Little One barely the age of a fuzzy pouf flower to do this. We have lost our minds."

Holly exhaled, afraid her new partner might be correct. "The Little One looks like one of the images on the cards. I think she is part of this too. She, umm, is also Bishop Ward's niece." Holly grimaced and braced for Asa's reaction.

"What? The orphaned baby from Yagora's cult sacrifice? The one whose parents—Ward's sister? Are you kidding me? Holly, I swear I could ... scream!" Asa stomped around the room, pulling at her ponytail. She looked like she wanted to hit something.

Holly put her small paws up. "Calm down. I did not know at the time."

Where is Yanka when you need her to subdue a Dark Fae? Holly thought. *Sheesh!*

"Oh, and that is supposed to make me feel better? How can we possibly trust her? There are so many factors at play."

"Asa, I understand your concern, but I have witnessed this Little One's interactions around the palace. She is trustworthy, and if the universe has chosen her, we must trust in the process."

"What is the universe thinking? We are trusting the fate of our prophecies to Little Ones who are barely as old as a wart on a troll's ass."

Holly jerked her head toward the lieutenant. "Lieutenant Asa, I expect that language from Lieutenant Zion, but not you."

Asa straightened. "I apologize. I gave him a long hug before we departed today—apparently some of his candor may have wiped off on me. It will pass."

"You are close?" Holly smirked.

Asa waved her hand dismissively. "Not like that, Holly, contrary to the rumors. While Lieutenant Zion and I are very close, we have never aura-blended, nor will we. I do not blend with any Fae. My gifts make it very difficult to do so. Besides, who would want to with me?" Asa turned around before Holly could say anything; clearly, she did not want to continue the conversation. "When Rowan comes here, then what?"

Holly followed her lead. "We rescue the Fae boy."

"And what? Bring him to Blood Haven? That is kidnapping! King Jarvok may not approve. Actually, I know he will not approve."

Holly shrugged. "Lady Zarya will explain. He will understand."

"And what if he does not?" Asa shot back. Holly knew this had more to do with Asa's fear of rejection than anything else. Asa had only recently given Jarvok her old Angelite disc as a sign of loyalty, and he, in turn, had fused it into his left arm. Asa was concerned she would lose her place with Jarvok.

"Let's worry about getting him out first. Worst case, Rowan and I can take him into the human world for safekeeping, along with Indiga," Holly said.

"We are taking the blue-eyed Little One too? If we take her with us, it's royal kidnapping, with different repercussions. She is the only ward of the Court of Light, which means technically she is Aurora's legacy. I remember hearing about her when Jarvok and Zion were discussing the Unity Contract. That Little One came up several times as a possible stumbling block for the line of succession. There exists a small pocket of Light Fae who think she has a claim to the throne. Do you understand how dangerous this is?" Asa's mask shifted as her brows shot up.

"All the more reason to take her with us. Tell me of one ruler who would want their challenger alive? Besides, from what I have seen, no Fae takes that Little One seriously. Trust me on that. More importantly, she was on the cards. I am telling you: she is wrapped up in all this." Holly pointed toward the door.

"Trust you? I am standing in the room where Geddes tried to strike you down just a few hours ago, and now we are discussing kidnapping and a jailbreak. We aren't running a camp for wayward Fae. This is complicated."

"Earth-shattering prophecies usually are. They are rarely neat and convenient."

Asa sucked in her cheeks. "Fine, just the blue-eyed Little One, no more. I'll have to figure something out to avoid war and kidnapping charges." She rubbed her temples.

"You are moving with the universe, my friend."

Asa paused, her fingertips still at her temples. "Yes, you tell King Jarvok that, and then make sure they put it on my memorial marker: 'Here lies Asa—she moved with the universe.' Ha, ha. What a troll's prick." She smacked her forehead.

Chapter Twenty-One:
All Is Not What It Seems.
It Never Is...

Nightshade relieved her fellow Illuminasqua standing guard over Lady Sybella's visiting quarters. Earlier, the guards had carried the Oracle in with Familiar Rowan's help. Two healers had come and gone per the last guard's report. Other than that, it had been quiet around her door. Desdemona had been concerned Bishop Geddes might try to disturb the Oracle with questions about the prophecies since he, the other bishops, Queen Sekhmet, and the Court of Dark had missed the readings. The misstep in protocol had never happened, but then again, nothing about the day had been normal.

Nightshade mulled over what she had learned and whom she had discovered things about. Some pieces of information were not new but now confirmed. She had always mistrusted the bishops, especially after their abrupt change in behavior when Queen Aurora announced her engagement.

The three bishops had become more withdrawn and isolated, Bishop Geddes most of all. He had a dislike for the Illuminasqua and their captain in particular; snide remarks about her lineage as a Power Angel were the norm in conversation. It seemed to slip the bishops' minds that without her Power Angel lineage and Desdemona's Elestial Blade, the Court of Light would not have stood a chance during the war. The fact was, without the Elestial Blade, their Harbinger blades could not have been forged, yet Desdemona never garnered one compliment. Desdemona had forged several different weapons with her Elestial Blade and used her light to charge them. Even so, the bishops and some of the Heads of Houses looked down upon her for starting her existence as a Power Angel.

Despite everything Nightshade already knew about Bishop Geddes, she was surprised to see how adamant he was about hearing the prophecies, so much so that he had tried to strike down the Court of Dark's Familiar. The mink was small, but her size did not match the power she held. Holly was not a creature to be taken lightly. But she had been in a vulnerable state at the time Geddes raised his staff to her; to attack her under those circumstances was particularly cruel.

Nightshade had been angry, but Desdemona was enraged. While Nightshade had witnessed her captain's temper firsthand in battle, this had been very different. Usually, Desdemona possessed exceptional control. Nightshade envied it. Desdemona might show a flash of emotion, but it would be gone quickly. In battle, it would be unleashed on her enemies, but her fighting was clean and efficient. Nightshade had done her fair share of killing. She knew the cold, quiet place the Illuminasqua went to in order to send another to their Oblivion. Nightshade would disconnect herself and wait for the sweet silence to engulf her, the screaming and pleading dampened as she took their light.

However, what she had seen on her captain's face was not cold disconnection; it was the opposite. Desdemona's fury was its own entity. It had invaded her aura and taken root. The outrage gave her eyes life, reminding Nightshade of a fire raging during a war. Those fires had a heartbeat that started when the first ember glowed—kindled in hate to destroy. They burned hot and out of control, as if the flames fed off the pain and loss. The screams and tears of those the inferno destroyed turned the sky into an orange haze. That was what had been in Desdemona's eyes: the orange, blues, and reds of an all-consuming fire. Whatever Desdemona had tapped into had always been there, but it had been restricted until now. She no longer had control over it. Nightshade was convinced it was not going back into its cage anytime soon. The notion made her uneasy, more so than breaking bread with Bishop Geddes, and that was saying something.

As Nightshade contemplated her next move, she kept watch over the Oracle's door and heard movement farther down the corridor. A whoosh of air alerted her to an Air elemental, and a second later, a small figure arrived in front of the door. She removed her hood in a smooth motion, revealing long golden-blond curls. Bishop Ward's niece Indiga was a precocious Fae, with no loyalty to her uncle, as he often only used her to garner sympathy; she was a reminder of his sorrow to parade around when it suited him. Let the universe bless her, because when he did such things, Indiga always found a way to get even.

There was one time which stuck in Nightshade's mind: Indiga had shown up to an event in literal rags after she overheard her uncle complaining about having to buy her a new dress because she was growing too fast, and what a burden she was on his wallet. Lady Navi, Head of the House of Pavonibus and the Peafowl (needless to say, how you looked was kind of a thing to them) had come into the shop moments later. Then Ward had switched to loud bragging: "Money is no object for my favorite niece." He had been trying to aura-blend with Lady Navi for months. Later, Ward had delivered the new dress to Indiga and thrown it on the bed, telling Ungarra, "You deal with her, she is not my responsibility."

Queen Aurora had heard all about the new dress from the bishop. He'd told her that he raised Indiga like a daughter. Indiga had taken umbrage at the blatant lie and shown up to the event wearing a potato sack. When asked why she had dressed like that, the Little One had replied, "It is punishment because I did not polish my uncle's staff properly. Now I am forced to dress like a troll." Indiga was aware of the double entendre. Ward tried to say he had bought her a dress, but the seamstress was on Indiga's side, as Ward had haggled with her on price and even demanded it be done for free because he was a bishop. The seamstress had seen him treat the Little One cruelly.

When Ward questioned the seamstress at the party, the seamstress merely shrugged. "I simply cannot remember if I made a dress for the Little One. I made so many for this event."

Indiga was escorted to her suite and no one saw her for days. Rumors swirled that she was healing from wind burn.

The entire palace staff was aware how much Ward despised Indiga and how he treated her; it was a horribly kept secret among them, but the Heads of Houses and even Aurora were none the wiser.

The staff would try to help Indiga when they could. Unfortunately, the Little One always paid the price.

Nightshade was confident Indiga was not there on any business of her uncle's, but that did not explain what she was doing visiting the Oracle. Indiga rapped on the door and bit her lower lip. She glanced around nervously.

Shrouded in shadow, Nightshade crouched down. "Why are you so anxious, Little One?" she murmured to herself.

Indiga knocked again, bouncing on her toes. "Come on, come on ... open up ... open up..." Indiga breathed. Suddenly, she raised her hands like she had remembered something. Her mouth made a perfect *O* shape, and she looked up with her tongue stuck to her top lip as she dug around in her pocket and produced a small, folded piece of parchment. She slid it under the door. Indiga bounced faster, filled with excitement and anxiety. A moment later the door creaked open and Indiga's face lit up; she gave an over-animated wave, pleasantries were exchanged, and she nodded, seeming to accept an invite inside.

Pulling up her hood, Nightshade had mere seconds to react. Expertly, she slid in behind Indiga. Neither the Little One nor the room's occupant noticed her.

As the door closed, a breeze caught Indiga's blond curls across her face. She fixed her hair and found Rowan the champagne fox smiling at her.

"Hello, my blueberry muffin. My, what big eyes you have. I see we need to talk," he said, holding up the Oracle's card depicting E. The fox was smart enough to keep it facing him.

"Holly sent me. She is in the Contemplation Room, ah ... the *Reading Room* with the Dark Fae with the pretty blue hair. She asked me to tell you to go to her, and she would like it if you could also bring a cloak, please." Indiga gave him a gigantic smile, proud she had remembered the full message.

Rowan nodded. "I see, thank you. Let me find a cloak, and we will be on our way. Wait here." He left the room to speak with Lady Sybella.

The sweet aroma of roses wafted through the room as Rowan knocked softly on the door to Lady Sybella's chambers and entered. The afternoon light diffused through the pink drapes hanging on the arched windows, casting a feminine glow over the Light Oracle's bedroom. The large canopy was bathed in swathes of light-pink and sage-green silk fabric. The bed was made of teak with ivy vines carved into the wood, as though the ivy was wrapped around the four posters. Green watermelon tourmaline crystals occupied the center of the cherry rose sculptures blooming at the top of each poster. The headboard had an intricately designed septagram carved into the wood; inlaid crystals represented each element. The side table held a crystal decanter of spring water and various tonics from the healers. Raw crystals had been placed at the bottom of a drinking glass.

Large pieces of sunstone were laid out around her bed to help balance her aura, and alchemic glyphs were drawn on the floor to aid in its cleansing. Lady Sybella lay above the sumptuous blush-colored bed linens, awake but deep in thought, holding her prophecy stone. The reading had been an event in itself, but her eyes changing was something altogether unexpected. A short time after the reading, Rowan had noticed her right pupil had morphed into the shape of the sun, and her left pupil had become a star. This was a sign from Mother Luna, but he did not tell her that it meant she would be claimed by the Shadow Realm upon her death. He was positive Lady Zarya was claimed as well. He recalled how jarring it was when it happened to him; it was seen as a mark of the demon, and it sealed his fate, or rather, resulted in the death of his human body. Now of course, he knew better; therefore, he told Lady Sybella it meant her gifts had expanded, which was a partial truth. Her gifts had indeed grown, but there was no need to explain the Shadow Realm or Mother Luna. Those were mysteries he was not at liberty to share yet. The idea of immortality was overwhelming for many, and she had been through enough today. Rowan was positive Holly would be taking the same approach with Zarya.

When she did not respond to his knocks, Rowan cleared his throat. "My Lady?"

She did not look up. "Yes, Rowan, I know you must leave me now," she said flatly.

Her response caught him off guard. He shook his head. "I will not be long. I must assist Holly on a quick errand. That is all."

Lady Sybella did not flinch. "It will be more complicated and longer than you think, my fox."

He hated leaving her. He had grown very fond of the Oracle. Before he could protest, there was a sneeze behind him. He turned to see Indiga wiping her nose on her sleeve and very much in the Oracle's bedroom. "I thought I told you to stay put, muffin?" he said, an edge to his voice.

Indiga looked down and shuffled her feet.

Lady Sybella broke the awkward silence. "Merry Meet, Indiga."

Indiga snapped to attention and remembered her manners. She bowed to the Oracle. "Merry Meet, Lady Sybella. I am sorry to bother you. I hope you are feeling well," the small Fae said in a meek voice.

Sybella smiled. "You are no bother, Indiga, not to me or to anyone. Remember that, Little One."

Indiga blushed. "Yes, ma'am."

"May I speak with Rowan before you two go on your adventure, please?" the Oracle asked. Indiga smiled at *adventure*.

"Yup! I mean, yes, ma'am, and thank you." She bowed and left the room.

Sybella shook her head and smiled. She motioned for Rowan to come closer. "Do you have the picture cards, my fox?"

Rowan tilted his head up toward her. "Yes, my lady." He pulled them out, figuring she wanted them before he left, but she stopped him.

"Keep them. They are meant for her."

Rowan was utterly confused now. "Her?"

The Oracle lifted her chin, motioning toward the door. "The Little One is the reader we saw in the prophecy. When she is ready, you must show her how to use them. Promise me you will, my fox."

Rowan shook his head in disbelief. "The little blueberry muffin is the reader?"

Sybella curled her lips. "Yes, my fox, she is. *A wind rider becomes the reader.* Now go—your friend needs you. A new journey awaits." She hugged him close, his fur warm on her face. Rowan smelled like the forest: clean, crisp mountain air mixed with the earthy scent of pine needles. She loved it, and she knew it would be a while before it enveloped her again.

He pulled away and found her eyes welling up. "I'll be back in no time, my lady," Rowan said with the utmost confidence.

She pulled him in for one more hug.

"Oh, may I borrow a cloak?" he asked.

"Of course," she said with a weak smile.

Rowan pulled a red velvet cloak from her armoire. "This one. It is one of your Dresser's cloaks. Is that all right?"

"It will work better for you, Rowan. Trust me," Sybella replied, blinking back her tears.

"Thank you, my favorite lady."

"You are welcome, my favorite fox."

Rowan winked as he reached for his plumed hat and shut the door to her bedroom.

"Be careful, my fox. You have no idea what you are walking into," the Oracle whispered with only the empty room to hear her.

In the sitting room, Rowan found Indiga perched on the chaise couch, swinging her feet. He waved the red velvet cloak and tossed it to her to carry, "Let's go, my blueberry muffin."

Indiga hopped down from the couch. The two headed out, unaware Nightshade was following close behind them.

Chapter Twenty-Two:
LITTLE BIG MOUTH

Careful to avoid the patrolling palace guards, the fox and the little Fae arrived at the door to the Reading Room. Most of the excitement of the day was dying down, and the halls of the palace had returned to their normal pace. A few Fae were prepping for evening rituals and dinner. Indiga rapped on the door and slipped inside. She glanced around the room, but no one was there.

"I swear they were here." Her cheeks puffed out with her rapid breathing. "I am not making up tales, Rowan. I promise."

Rowan hushed her with a graze of his tail. "Shh, blueberry muffin. It's okay." The fox sniffed the room as he padded inside. "Holly, luv I am here. Come out, come out, wherever you are," he sang.

The air shimmered directly in front of Rowan and Indiga as Holly manifested there. "Rowan," Holly said breathlessly.

Asa stepped out from the balcony.

"Nice trick. I forgot you could do that." Rowan exhaled with relief.

Holly braced herself against his front leg, exhausted. "Yes, but I can do it very sparingly."

Rowan supported the mink, turning his eyes toward Asa. "Lieutenant Asa, long time no see. I gather the cloak is for you." He motioned for Indiga to hand the red velvet cloak to the Dark Fae.

Asa nodded. "Thank you."

Rowan stood back as Holly collected her resolve. "So, what is going on? Am I so irresistible that you could not bear to be away from me?" He smiled wryly, twitching his whiskers.

Holly shook her head. "Lady Zarya sent us to find E— apparently the Fae is much more important to the prophecies than anyone could have imagined. Along with the others," Holly added in a low tone.

"Others?" Confusion crossed Rowan's furry face. "What others?" He knew of Indiga's future as the reader, but he needed time to speak with Holly and piece this together. "Holly, we need to talk, love."

"One second, Rowan." Holly's tone turned commanding.

"No Holly, *now* ... and where is E? Holly! Look at me!" He puffed out his cheeks, annoyed at her dismissive attitude.

Holly put her paw up to Rowan. "Hush!"

Rowan's head snapped around. "Excuse me?"

"You can come out of hiding, Illuminasqua. I know you are here!" Holly said aloud.

Asa drew her blade. Most of the room flinched as the Auric weapon's light cast long shadows on the walls.

Indiga didn't give the blade a second look. The fox glanced at her with newfound respect but quickly turned his attention back to the invisible intruder. He sniffed the air, catching her scent. "We know you are here, Illuminasqua," Rowan said.

Indiga took it upon herself to deal with the problem directly. "Look, we aren't plotting against the crown, but if my uncle has something to do with this, I will not let him get away with it!" she spat. Her arms away from her body, she slowly rotated in a taunting display of come-and-get-me. The little Fae had a sneer, daring the Illuminasqua to show herself.

Holly's eyes widened.

Asa looked down at the petite Fae and back at Holly. "Plucky or careless, I can't tell, but I think I like her."

Nightshade appeared on the balcony. *They don't need to know where I came from or how I got in,* she thought. The Illuminasqua pushed the door open and strode through with an air of authority. "What is the meaning of this, Lieutenant Asa? Captain Desdemona gave you safe passage out of the Court of Light, yet you return. Why?" Nightshade placed her hands on her hips; she felt an answer was due.

Asa met her halfway. "I am not going to try to deceive you. I am an honorable Fae." *Honesty is my best option.* "There is a small Fae in danger. The Oracles have sent us back to rescue him from your cells. That is the truth, Illuminasqua." She sheathed her blade, and the overexaggerated shadows disappeared, leaving the room feeling empty.

Nightshade snorted. "She speaks the truth," Rowan said. "Both Oracles said he is the key to the prophecies."

Nightshade glanced about the room. "No one heard the prophecies today, Asa. Where is the boy?" She folded her arms in defiance.

"Lady Zarya relayed the Dark prophecy, and it was complicated, to say the least," Asa said. "I told you: the little Fae is in the cells. He is being held there."

The co-captain of the elite force shook her head. "Impossible. The Illuminasqua would know if any Fae, regardless of age, was being held in the cells. That is under our jurisdiction. The only reason to hold a Fae would be for protective custody, which is the job of the Illuminasqua." She returned to her power pose, legs apart, hands on her hips and shoulders back.

Rowan paced, his tail swaying. "Would they, muffin? Your captain was stripped of her command. Your Bishop Geddes tried to strike down a Familiar while demanding the Court of Dark's prophecy stone, something he knows he has no right to. Do you really believe the Illuminasqua are in the loop? By the way, when was the last time you saw your captain? Did you see her after she tangoed with the bishop?"

Nightshade's face remained expressionless. "So, what do you expect me to do, Familiar Rowan? Let you waltz into the cells and rescue a Fae who may or may not be there? That could be seen as treason!"

While she longed to interject, Asa understood that this was not her battle. She remained silent.

However, Indiga sauntered up to the second-in-command of the much-feared Illuminasqua. "No one asked for you to *let* us do anything! Nor did we ask for your help! You inserted yourself into this, and frankly, you can take yourself right back out." Indiga made a little power pose of her own, fists on her hips, feet apart and puffed out her chest to match Nightshade's.

Asa almost choked on her own laughter, covering her mouth as the little Fae spoke.

Rowan stepped in front of Indiga to calm the situation. "I think what my blueberry muffin is trying to say is, while we appreciate your help—"

But Indiga cut the fox off, bumping him with hip as she took her place right back in front of Nightshade. "Forgive me, Rowan, but this little muffin can speak for herself. I meant what I said! We don't need her help, and we didn't ask for it. My best friend E is stuck in a cell because we were playing hide and seek in the palace. My uncle can be a big old bag of wind, and if he caught E..." She bit her lip, trying to hold on to her anger. "E is in big trouble. We will find him on our own. Go back to your captain. You have never trusted the bishops. Believe me, my uncle hates the Illuminasqua, so get out of our way so we can find E. You never saw us, and we never saw you, no treason. Problem solved. Buh-bye." She waved to Nightshade, then flicked her wrist to open the door.

Rowan gestured to Asa to close the door, not wanting to attract any nosy passersby.

Indiga turned her back to the Illuminasqua and faced Holly. "So, how do we get to the cells?" she asked as if Nightshade was no longer in the room.

Asa shook her head in disbelief at Indiga's brashness. "Can someone please explain to me *who* this Little One is, besides being E's best friend?" Asa jerked her thumb at the Fae.

Nightshade took the liberty of answering. "Lieutenant Asa, met Indiga Corrianda Ward, Bishop Ward's niece, otherwise known around the palace as Little Big Mouth."

Oh, that's right, I did hear the guard call her that, Holly thought. *Guess the name is well deserved. It's a little harsh, but considering what I just witnessed, not far off.*

Indiga folded her arms with a sardonic smile.

"Proud of it?" Asa inquired of the little Fae.

Indiga spun on her heels to face her. "It may be the Court of Light, but it is hard to survive here." The little powerhouse's cerulean eyes resembled a tumultuous sea, the pounding waves shaping the shoreline. Asa knew that no matter her size, age, or cuteness, this one had seen her share of pain.

Indiga's tapping foot echoed on the crystal floor. "Can we get back to figuring out how we are rescuing my best friend?"

Nightshade caved, putting her arms up. "I will take my leave. I will not alert anyone to your presence, but..." She swept her arm around the room, to encompass them all. "I will not defend you either. Lieutenant Asa, protect Little Big Mouth. She is just a Little One despite what comes out of that mouth." She closed her hand around the hilt of one of her Harbinger swords. "If something happens to her, I will see that you pay dearly."

Asa nodded in acknowledgment.

Indiga stuck her tongue out at Nightshade, who rolled her eyes and smirked. The Illuminasqua took one last look at the quartet before closing the door.

Nightshade stood on the other side of the door, her hand resting on the cool wood. *I am not comfortable with this, but Rowan brought up a good point. I have not heard from Desdemona since the incident in the Contemplation/ Reading Room.* There was one place Desdemona liked to go when she wanted to be alone: the Crystal Causeways. *Whatever these guys are up to is not my concern right now.* She pulled up her hood and disappeared down the hall.

Chapter Twenty-Three:
SCARS CAN HEAL

"C an we get back to finding E?" Indiga stomped her feet, her hands balled up into fists.

Asa glanced out the window. "Little Big—*Indiga* is correct. We need to move. Rowan, how far are we from the cells?"

Rowan paced the room. "I am afraid we are quite far from the entrance. They are literally on the other side of the palace grounds, and then we must go underground. Indiga and I can navigate, but you, my Dark Fae, even with the cloak, will be a hard sell." Rowan sat, placing his hat back on his head. "There is a shortcut, but I can't see how it is possible; it would put us in full view."

"Where is the shortcut?" Asa asked.

Rowan motioned for them to look outside the windows. "The path to Oblivion. The doors they led Aurora out of today—that stairwell leads to the cells. We would have to cross the courtyard at dusk, when every Fae is getting ready for evening rituals. How can we do that with you in tow, my burnt muffin?" Rowan eyed Asa up and down. "The cloak will not hide the outline of your armor—it is fine for the lonely corridors but not the gossips in the courtyard."

Indiga smiled. "I have an idea! Asa, can you please remove your helmet so I can see your hair?" Asa glanced at Holly, who shrugged. Indiga looked up at Asa with pleading eyes. Asa did as she was told but lowered her head so that her hair fell in her face. She kept her mask on.

No one commented on Asa leaving her mask in place.

Indiga clapped. "Okay, sit on the couch," she commanded, and Asa obliged. The Little One got to work braiding Asa's light-blue hair, pulling it away from her face, working around the mask. A few minutes later, the little Fae had whipped it up into a long fishtail braid. "There! When she puts the hood on, no one will see her hair. She is my new nanny!"

"You know what, Little One? You might be on to something," Rowan said. He handed Asa the red velvet cloak.

"I can still see her armor, but without her helmet, it is much better," Holly said as Asa slipped it on.

They all turned at the sound of rustling in the corner of the room. Indiga had practically crawled into the armoire—all they could see were her little feet sticking out as she threw garments over her shoulder. Finally, she emerged victorious, holding up two long dresses: one pink and one light green. "Ta-da! Aurora always kept extra dresses for humans that requested an audience with her, so they would be properly dressed. We can put her in one of these."

Rowan and Holly shrugged at each other. "Let us give it a try, muffin."

Asa spoke up. "No! I will not remove my armor."

Indiga's face fell.

"For this to work, Lieutenant Asa, we cannot have Kyanite stalagmites or skull outlines protruding from underneath the cloak," Holly said.

Asa knew they were correct; she glanced down at the cloak and could see her armor sticking out. *Troll's balls, goblin's prick, and everything in between—I am going to have to wear a dress. Should have had Zion take Zarya back. He probably would have looked great in a dress. what do the humans say? Fick? Yeah, that's it. Fick my life.* "Fine," Asa grumbled after much mental debate, gritting her teeth.

"Right, love. Indiga, grab the pink," Rowan said. Asa cleared her throat. "I mean the *green*. Bring it here. Good choice; it goes with your hair," he said sheepishly as Indiga ran over, holding the green silk dress.

Asa kept her head down, still trying to shield her face, and stepped behind the billowing balcony curtains to give herself some privacy. She carefully took her Kyanite armor off piece by piece: first unfastening each skull-covered shoulder pauldron, then the gorget, which ran to right under her chin. The gorget had three purple and gold ametrine crystals running down the center. She smiled as she ran her fingers over them. They were gifts from Zion. He had given them to her because they promoted mental clarity and could cleanse one's aura. *Zion could use some mental enhancement,* she thought, stifling a giggle. Asa kissed the crystals. *I'll see him soon.* Next, she unfastened her chest piece and slipped off her leather pants. Asa placed the armor pieces off to the side, stacking them neatly. She stared at her gauntlets, the last remnants of Kyanite besides her mask. She rubbed at the battle-worn protectors, her fingers getting caught in the grooves, reminders of fights won. For some reason, she didn't want to let these go; it was like giving up that portion of her life. They had saved her so many times. *This is ridiculous, I'll get them back. I'll get all this back. I'll have Zion come for them. Why am I acting like I am never going to put this back on? Ugh, cut it out.*

Asa removed the gauntlets and laid them on top of the pile. She slipped into the green-hued dress, adjusting the neckline so it lay flat against her skin. She pulled up a swath of silk chiffon attached at the waist to wrap around her neck. She inspected the stitching on the side of the dress and took a small knife from her boot to cut a slit from the bottom hem to mid-thigh so she could move unencumbered. *Nothing I can do about the boots—I cannot go barefoot. Perhaps the cloak will be enough to conceal them if I hold it closed.* She took a breath and swung her long braid over her shoulder, then slid the stack of armor from behind the curtain. "Can you put this behind the couch, please?" She lingered, not ready to reveal her new look.

Indiga and Rowan pulled the couch away from the wall to conceal the armor behind it. Strategically, the Familiars piled the armor, and Indiga adjusted the dust ruffle to conceal it if someone happened to look underneath. As the fox finished placing the final pieces, he discovered that there was one missing.

"The mask, please, Lieutenant Asa," Rowan called to her in a compassionate tone. "And your footwear—we will find you slippers from the armoire. We can't have you thumping around in Kyanite boots with a silk gown."

He turned to Indiga. "Find her slippers or something, please."

Indiga gave him two thumbs up and dove back into the armoire to look for more appropriate footwear.

Asa was going to protest about the boots but realized it was probably a good idea to switch them out. Besides, it delayed her removing her mask.

A few heartbeats passed, and Indiga slid a delicate pair of gold slippers with matching gold threading beneath the curtain. "Thank you," Asa called, putting them on. The shoes were a little snug, so she stretched and pointed her feet to try to break them in. These were not like anything she would even think to wear, but they did look much better than her Kyanite boots.

Then came the moment she had dreaded. Asa's hands shook as she reached behind her head to unfasten the ties. The leather and Black Kyanite crystal camouflage had been part of her for as long as she could remember. It felt heavy in her hands; she had not realized its weight. Asa touched her face, running her fingers over her skin. The scars did not have a different texture from the rest of her skin, but she knew they were there. Her face had not been exposed like this in centuries. She had not kept track of her new disfigurements; she was aware of them but avoided mirrors at all costs. Unfortunately, there would be three sets of eyes looking at her now. Sometimes, that was worse than a mirror.

Asa stepped out from her makeshift dressing room. Gone was the Dark Fae warrior, replaced by a lady of the Court of Light.

"Asa, you look amazing," Holly said.

"The gown fits you impeccably," Rowan noted as he walked around her. "It hugs your waist and accentuates your toned warrior physique, which no one would never know you had in your Kyanite armor. The green contrasts the highlights in your blue hair; it makes the turquoise stand out."

Indiga giggled, and the room looked at her. "What?" Her hands went up. "Rowan sounds like the gossips by the reflecting pools before evening rituals, only what he said was nice. They never say nice things about what the other Fae are wearing." She shrugged.

Holly smirked. "Rowan does sound like a gossiping gape-mouthed fish sometimes, doesn't he?"

Rowan twitched. "Well, excuse me for appreciating fashion." He flicked his plumed velvet hat.

Both Holly and Indiga laughed. "Oh, is that fashion?" Indiga teased in a mock English accent.

Asa cleared her throat. Not that she was looking for the attention, but they were on a schedule. Everyone returned their attention to the Dark Fae.

"You do look lovely, Asa," Holly said.

Rowan doffed his hat and gave her a sweeping bow. "If Zion could see you now..."

Asa blushed, tugging at the gown's bust line. "How do you expect me to fight in this?" She did a few practice punches and the gown shifted. She stepped farther into the light.

Indiga stared at her scars, then hurriedly looked away.

Asa caught Indiga staring again. "Ask me, Little One. I do not believe you earned your nickname because you like holding back." She braced for the inevitable.

Indiga's small mouth pursed as if she was searching for the right wording. "Did someone hurt you?"

Holly's head jerked back. The phrasing of the question had caught the mink off guard. "What do you mean hurt her?" She kept her tone calm, non-judgmental.

Indiga bit her lip and fiddled with her hands. "Well ... her scars, they, umm ... look like mine, and I know how I got mine." She dropped her gaze to her feet.

Holly glanced at Rowan, who tilted his chin, urging her onward.

"Yours?" Holly asked, scampering up the little Fae's body.

Indiga's curls covered her face as she bobbed her head up and down.

"May I see them?" Holly whispered, moving the little Fae's hair from her eyes. Indiga nodded and Holy jumped down. The Little One removed her coat and slipped the back of her green-and-blue flower-print dress from her shoulders to the middle of her back. Long and short scars crisscrossed her pink skin. They were in various states of healing, some only a few days old. Some were years old.

Rowan closed his eyes tightly, the tears welling up.

Suddenly, Asa was slammed with the emotional remnants of the damage left under the Little One's skin. She did her best to control the anger.

Holly sucked in her cheeks, trying not to let Indiga sense her own rage. The mink patted the little Fae's leg while she covered back up. "Your uncle did this." It was not a question, but a statement made through gritted teeth.

Indiga didn't speak but a nod of the head was all they needed.

Asa bent down and tried to take Indiga's hands in hers. Indiga did not move, so Asa tucked her fingers under the Little One's chin, raising Indiga's head until their eyes met.

Indiga gave her a tight-lipped grin. "I like your white eye. It reminds me of a snowball. E and I had wonderful snowball fights."

She said it so innocently that Rowan choked up, turning his head away so as to not interrupt their moment.

Asa had forgotten about her eyes; to anyone else they could be jarring, but this little Fae found them pretty. "Indiga, my whole body is covered in scars." Indiga's eyes widened as Asa stuck out her arms. "See?" Indiga felt Asa's skin with her fingertips. The scars looked like twisted rope strangling her skin. They had an iridescent glow all their own and appeared to be moving beneath Asa's flesh, suffocating her light and robbing her of love and relationships. The scars were not as thick on Asa's face. They were smooth and, in a pattern, which reminded the little Fae of *something*. She traced the marks on the Dark Fae's right cheek. Asa closed her eyes. It was the first time she had let anyone this close to her in centuries.

"I think your scars are beautiful, like a spider's web," Indiga whispered. Asa opened her eyes and realized Indiga was beaming, her bright eyes almost glowing.

She held the Little One's hand. "Thank you, Indiga. No one has ever said those words to me. Our scars do not define us, no matter how we got them. They are proof we went through a storm and survived."

Indiga's mouth scrunched up like she was trying to remember something. Suddenly she nodded as the thought came to her. "Queen Aurora told me Lady Serena said every Fae is beautiful inside and out. Oh, and every girl should wear an invisible crown. I'm not sure about the last part, but I understand the first."

Asa laughed softly. "I think you are beautiful inside and out, Indiga. No one should ever hit you, and after we find E, I want you to come with me. I will protect you, and no one will ever hurt you again." *I have no idea how I am going to do this but leaving Indiga is not an option. Her uncle will wind-burn her again, and I will not allow it. I do not care about royal kidnapping charges or whether Jarvok will understand. Indiga is coming with me, end of discussion. Oh, by all that is light in the universe, what am I doing? I am doing what is right.*

Indiga gave her the biggest smile. "We can go together? Truly? We can tell each other we're pretty and have adventures?" She wrapped her arms around Asa's neck and hugged her.

"Yes, Little One, and you can meet my dragon, Yanka."

Indiga jumped up and down, still holding on to Asa. "You have a *dragon*?" She stepped back, her expression serious. "Do you happen to know anyone who deals in large butterflies?" Asa gave her a quizzical look, not understanding.

Holly choked up, watching the two.

Rowan bumped his hip against the mink's. "Holly, are you crying, luv?" he teased.

"No! Allergies. When was the last time you bathed, fox?" she curtly replied. She bumped him back. "Asa, can we please get on with things?"

"We have a courtyard to storm," Rowan said.

Chapter Twenty-Four:
TRY TO BLEND

T he sage-green silk dress easily transformed the Dark Fae warrior into a member of the Court of Light. Asa had never worn silk. She only knew the Kyanite armor and her linen sleepwear. This was the first time since she was a small Glimmer in the Shining Kingdom, before she took her Power Angel oath, that she had worn anything different. The fabric felt foreign to her, even though the silk was soft and fluid against her skin. It might as well have been sandpaper. Without her Kyanite armor and the grounding properties of the black crystal, she was bombarded with the emotions of the room: unease, worry, fear, hero worship (*That must be Indiga*, she thought), and hope.

Asa stumbled back, reaching for something to steady her. She took a breath and consciously aligned her Chakras. Picturing the colorful globes of swirling energy deep within her body, she called upon them one-by-one. She imagined them glowing and spinning at the same brightness and speed, and once she was positive that they were all equally charged, she recited: *"My emotional and energetic boundaries are strong. My body reacts to my energy. My aura listens to my words. My shields are raised and they obey. One song, one truth.*"

Asa's white eye glowed and dimmed. She asked for her cloak. "I am ready. Let us leave," she said coldly. She covered her head with the scarlet hood, pulling it down past her face. Asa joined her hands together and tried to look subservient and meek.

Indiga stuck her head out of the slightly opened door. She glanced right and left down the hall. "All clear," she whispered, creeping out of the room. "We should take the back stairs. It will lead us to the kitchen and out to the courtyard."

"I believe Indiga's ruse about Asa being the nanny will suit us rather well," Rowan said. "Indiga, the kitchen will be crowded with preparations going on for the evening meal. We will need you to be a bit unruly, as if the new nanny is being broken in; no one will have an opportunity to ask us too many questions."

The little Fae winked at the fox. "One pain in a troll's ass, coming up!" she said a bit too enthusiastically. Already in character, the Little One tore off ahead of everyone

"Here goes everything," Rowan whispered.

The palace seemed calmer after the morning's commotion. A few Fae nodded at Rowan or gave greeted Indiga, but no one paid any mind to the Fae in the red cloak.

As the group approached the back stairs leading down to the kitchen, Indiga picked up her pace and began giggling. "No, I don't want to take a bath before evening ritual!" she shouted.

The hustle and bustle of the kitchen became louder as they approached. Cook shouted commands while pots and pans clanged.

"Go for it," Holly whispered from inside the little Fae's coat.

"I said no! Ha, ha, ha, you can't catch me!" Indiga stuck her tongue out as she skipped down the stairs.

Rowan followed suit. "Now, Indiga, stop giving her so much trouble. She has only been on the job a day," he said, making sure he could be heard by the entire kitchen staff.

Indiga ran through the kitchen, knocking anything over she could find, with Rowan and the new "nanny" close behind her. The little Fae ran directly into Cook and bounced off the Gnome's rather large belly.

"Little Big Mouth! What are you up to?" Cook bellowed.

Indiga smirked and grabbed an apple donut from the wooden chopping table. "Thanks, Cook!" She floated up and kissed the Gnome on the cheek, then glanced over her shoulder at her pursuers and took off. Cook turned to see Rowan and another Fae running through her kitchen.

"And where do you be thinkin' you are off to, Mr. Rowan?" the Gnome asked.

Rowan came to a halt. "Why, Cook, aren't you looking absolutely lovely this evening."

The Gnome was not buying it. She tapped her foot and the wooden spoon in unison. "I'll be having none of that sweet talk, fox," she said. "And who be this one?" She squinted and pointed her spoon at Asa.

"Beauty and brains. My, what a gift you are! This is Indiga's new nanny, only been here a few hours, and to be honest, muffin, trying not to get Bishop Ward upset after the day he has had, if you know what I mean. Hate for the poor thing to lose her head on her first day." Rowan feigned concern.

"Just go get Little Big Mouth. I won't be tellin'." Cook rolled her eyes.

Rowan kissed her hand. "You are such a gem!" The Gnome blushed. "I knew I could count on the most talented cook this side of the Veil," Rowan said, holding her hand a moment longer, the cook's green complexion deepening.

"Oh, Mr. Rowan," she cooed as he blew another kiss in her direction and ran out the side door.

They all met up outside the kitchen, next to a heap of flour bags and a wheelbarrow that provided the perfect cover for them to survey the busy courtyard. It was now early dusk, and the courtyard was bustling with Fae prepping for their evening rituals. The reflecting pools were a popular meeting place for members of the Houses to sit and gossip, and given what had transpired that day, the pools were overflowing with gossipmongers. A rose quartz obelisk had already been erected in the place where Aurora was executed.

"Damn, the Spelaions work fast," Indiga mumbled as the others turned to look at her. "What? Oh, come on. You were all thinking it. I just said it out loud!"

Rowan tilted his head. "Your nickname is well earned, Little One."

Asa scanned the area; the blue torches Rowan had pointed out from the Reading Room were lit, and she followed them to the large doors beyond. "I see the doors, Rowan, but judging by how crowded this area is, it's going to be hard not to attract attention. How are we going to slip inside without anyone noticing? I am also sure they are locked."

Holly peeked out of Indiga's coat. She noticed an open window to the side of the doors. *Most likely a guard's watch point—perfect for a small, flexible creature to slip through.* "I can get in through the window to the left of the doors and open them for you. Get me close and I will make a run for it, but we will need a distraction once I get the door open so that you Fae can run in."

They all agreed. It was too late to turn back now. The distraction would be figured out as they got closer.

"Try to blend," Rowan whispered to Asa as they walked with Indiga between them. They strolled past the reflecting pools, and the whispers started immediately. Fae pointed at Indiga, snickering and snorts of derision doggedly following their every step. "Not a word, Indiga," Rowan reminded the Little One.

"Ignore them," Holly said from inside her coat.

Asa could hear the rude commentary, the judgments about Indiga, and she very badly wanted to pull her blade out and show these Fae some manners. She had a new-found respect for what Indiga went through every day.

For all their snide remarks about Indiga, they were nothing but respectful to Rowan. "Merry Meet, Familiar Rowan!" many voices called to him. The fox tipped his chin in acknowledgment, but he did not break his stride.

There is no way any Fae would take Indiga seriously as a challenger for the throne, judging by the way she is treated. Asa wondered if Indiga was aware of the rumors about her viability as a successor—or if Ward was.

The group had cleared the second reflecting pool when a voice rang out, "Little Big Mouth! What have you done with my cousin?" E's cousin Amadora blocked their path, her evergreen cloak rustling in the breeze. She removed her hood, and her long hair swayed, matching the movement of her cape. While she looked like a fifteen-year-old human girl, that meant nothing on this side of the Veil; she could be twenty-five earth years old, it all depended on her faction. Amadora looked like she was skating around the precipice of adulthood. Her face had lost its cherubic fullness, and her high cheekbones were coming into their own, angular and sharp. Her eyes were feline in shape, large with a slight upturn at the edges. Amadora would be an unconventional beauty someday. Some might call her striking, while for others she might be a muse. She turned those eyes on Indiga. "E's mother went home in hysterics. I have been here all day searching for him. Where is he?"

The Fae around them stared and whispered. Indiga froze, unsure how to handle this new wrinkle. She looked to Rowan, her bottom lip trembling.

"Well, well aren't you lovely, all protective," Rowan remarked. "The chocolate hair with auburn highlights, and those eyes of yours ... gold with red flecks, yes, you are a sight. Well, my lovely muffin, Indiga here is with her new nanny. We are in a bit of a hurry, so if you don't mind, we will be on our way." He attempted to sidestep E's cousin, but she mirrored him as if they were dancing partners.

"Do not call me muffin, fox. I am not going anywhere, and neither are you until I get some answers," Amadora said, her voice growing louder.

Asa noticed the crowd was paying more attention. *Enough of this.* She dropped Indiga's hand and marched over to the Fae causing the ruckus. "Indiga is with us, so I suggest you move, Fae, or else I will make you." Her voice was low but menacing. She reached for the Fae's arm, but E's cousin snatched her arm away before Asa could apply pressure.

"Are you threatening me? You are nothing more than palace staff and should know your place," Amadora said in a haughty tone.

"We do not have time for this!" Holly said from inside Indiga's cloak, which Amadora overheard, mistaking the commentary for one of Indiga's snarky remarks.

She spun to face the little Fae. "Time for what, Indiga?" She reached for the Little One, but Asa interceded and grabbed her wrist, pressing the gold and red chrysanthemum vine bracelet into her skin.

"Let go of me! How dare you," Amadora spat out.

Asa pulled her close. "Shut up and listen, you simpering troll's ass. Amadora, is it? Walk with us if you want to see your cousin alive!" the Dark Fae hissed. Amadora clamped her mouth shut and nodded. "Your cousin is being held against his will. We are all trying to help get him out."

Amadora was not quick to believe such things, but Indiga's uncharacteristic behavior made the stranger's story plausible. She stared at Indiga, and the Little One gave a subtle nod without any acerbic retorts.

Amadora's face paled, and her knees buckled. Asa held the Fae up without much effort, grabbing her around her waist.

"Just call me Dora. E is a good Fae, a gentle Fae." Her eyes turned glassy, highlighting the tinges of red in her irises, like coals just on the verge of igniting. She rubbed at her wrist, straightening her bracelet.

Rowan tried to soothe her. "Hush, please, muffin. E overheard the Oracles' prophecies, and he was taken. I beg you, my lovely, keep walking." Rowan nodded affably to anyone who glanced in their direction as though they were merely discussing the weather.

Dora looked sharply at Indiga. "You had something to do with this! You are always causing trouble for my cousin!" Her whisper still managed to sound like acid dripping from her tongue.

Asa pulled Dora in closer toward her. "No! It was not her fault! Shut up, or else none of us will be able to help him." Dora quieted, but it did not stop her from glaring at the Little One.

The fab five loitered ten feet from the Pathway to Oblivion. The torches would burn throughout most of the night to signify that the execution had taken place. They would have no cover to sneak to the doors.

"Why is the Familiar involved? Did you talk to the queen?" Dora asked.

Indiga bent down, pretending to fix her shoes, and Holly climbed out from her coat.

"Thank you, Indiga," Holly said, and Rowan sat down to add coverage for Holly.

Dora jumped at the sight of the mink. "The Court of Dark's Familiar is here too?"

Asa gave Dora a deadpan glare. "That should tell you how serious this is. We believe the queen already knows, and that's why E is there." She backed up to complete the circle.

Holly eyed the window at the guard's checkpoint. "Rowan, have you come up with a distraction?"

Rowan sat back on his haunches, considering his options. He knew he could not blow Asa's cover too soon, so she was out. The red chrysanthemum vine on Dora's arm meant she was training to be a healer and had taken a vow to do no harm, so she was a no-go too.

"My little blueberry muffin, looks like the job falls to you," Rowan said, looking to Indiga. Her eyes grew large.

"What are you thinking?" Asa asked him, but instead of answering her, Rowan gestured toward the newly constructed rose quartz obelisk. He sighed with the knowledge of what he was going to ask Indiga to do. The pink plume of his hat arched forward, covering his mouth as he spoke into her ear. "My muffin, I need you to focus all of your elemental control to knock Aurora's memorial obelisk over. Do you think you can do that?"

Indiga put her thumb to her chin. "Umm .... I have never knocked over anything that big or heavy." She bit her lip.

Rowan kept his voice low and even. "I will help you. I can focus your call if you hold on to me while you channel your elemental power. Believe in yourself the way I do."

Asa stroked Indiga's hair, letting her fingers comb through the Little One's curls. "You can do this, Little Big Mouth," she said soothingly.

Dora folded her arms across her chest. "Of course she can. One thing I know about Indiga is that where she goes, destruction always follows." She gestured with her chin toward the obelisk. "This is *easy* for her." Dora gave Indiga a wink.

Holly did a double take at Dora's red flower bracelet. One of the images from the cards floated in her mind, and she stared up at the Fae, trying to remember if she was the face from the card. But before she could definitively say, Indiga's voice cut through, breaking her concentration.

"Get ready, mink, because here I go. One distraction coming up!"

Chapter Twenty-Five:
Did You Say Distraction or Destruction?

Rowan stood next to Indiga, his eyes closed. He concentrated, and when he opened his cold blue eyes, they had changed: his right pupil was a crescent moon and his left pupil was a star. Rowan had tapped into the Shadow Realm to help Indiga. "Oh, the fun we are about to have, my little blueberry muffin."

Indiga placed her left hand on the back of Rowan's neck and grounded herself.

"Give me to the count of ten to get inside, then bring it down," the mink said.

Rowan nodded. He could feel Indiga calling her element, Air, and his hackles rose. "Go, Holly!"

The mink scampered away, avoiding the crowd, and climbed up into the window, her paws digging into the crystal. She sighed as the torches' blue light poured over her fur. Their symbolism was not lost on her: only a few hours earlier, Aurora was alive, and now the torches glowed for the former queen's execution. The mink nimbly maneuvered through the cracked window without much difficulty. The post was empty, to her relief; the small door to the left of the stool where the guard must have sat took minimal effort to push open, and in a moment, she was in the tunnel that led deeper into the corridor.

Holly could see the dim light streaming in from the high-set windows. The path to the right would lead her back out to the courtyard. To her left was a long, dark corridor lit only by torches placed in sconces. She assumed this went toward the cells.

Holly ran her paw over the walls to find where the black tourmaline crystal started; this would verify the way toward the cells, no guessing. Black tourmaline had many advantages. It helped to block negative energies, repelled psychic attacks, and aided in the removal of negative energies within a Fae or, in this case, a space. However, one of the best reasons to use black tourmaline in a place such as this was to cleanse, purify, and transform dense energy into a lighter vibration, making an enemy more amenable to questioning. Aurora had done a fine job when she designed this facility. "I only hoped E is holding up well under the circumstances," Holly mumbled. "We go left. Got it," she said aloud to remind herself.

The mink began her next job, surveying the latches and locks. She stretched her arms. Luckily, besides being an expert lock picker, Holly had many otherworldly skills that made this job easy regardless of her short stature. She needed to use her supernatural tool belt and find the quickest way to do this. Holly concentrated and recited a phasing spell to reach into the lock mechanism and disengage the lock. "There, that was much easier than picking it," she said, waving her paw so that the lock returned to a corporeal state. "One down, two to go. Hope Rowan is on schedule out there. I wonder how long it takes to knock down an obelisk?"

Outside, Rowan was nearly done with his countdown: "...three, two, one."

Exhaling, Indiga bent her knees slightly and tightened her grip on Rowan's neck. She laced his soft, warm fur between her fingers until the two felt intertwined, like one unit of power. As she called the air around her, there was a prickle in her hand—or perhaps it had started *with* Rowan, the Little One wasn't sure. Her eyebrows crinkled. She could no longer tell where she began, and Rowan ended. The itching sensation traveled up from her hand and past her elbow, growing stronger inch by inch, and she shivered.

The air swirled around them. Rowan braced himself. He was impressed by how quickly Indiga had called her element.

The cool breeze brushed against Indiga's cheek as she lifted her right hand toward the obelisk. "Fall," she mouthed.

Asa and Dora provided cover so as not to arouse any more attention. "Come on, come on," Dora whispered, scanning the crowd, hoping no one noticed the little Fae.

A squall gathered at Indiga's feet, leaves dancing about. She felt a surge of power.

"What do you want?" a voice whispered into Indiga's ear. She was startled at first, but deep inside she recognized the breathy tone of the voice belonging to Air. She had heard her uncle speak to it before.

"Make it fall," she answered back.

"More specific, Little One, more specific," the voice said, sounding like the breeze on an autumn day.

Indiga huffed in exasperation. She was tired of holding her concentration this long. "The pink crystal structure. I need it to fall," she said through gritted teeth, though she didn't dare speak above a whisper. She was trying to not garner too much attention.

The air swirled again, moving her hair. "Why?" Now the voice sounded like a wintry howl.

The little Fae rolled her eyes behind her eyelids; even when concentrating she couldn't help it. "You sure ask a lot of questions for an elemental. I need a distraction. So, hurry up!" She stomped her foot.

The wind bayed, its laughter like a draft from within a deep cavern. "Release me, release your power, Little One, and I will obey. Tap into your throat Chakra. Speak my release."

Indiga grinned mischievously. She knew she did not have to yell or even raise her voice above a sigh to discharge her building energy. "I speak your release. *Vishuddha*." Her eyes flashed open and lit up, turning jade green as energy poured through her.

Dora gripped Asa's arm. The Dark Fae, without her Black Kyanite armor to block the energy surge, stiffened, feeling Indiga's power. "By all that is light in the universe..." Asa's tone was a mixture of suspense, anticipation, and surprise.

For a second, a pale turquoise cyclone materialized in the center of the crystal obelisk. The obelisk did not fall but exploded into hundreds of pieces. Dora ducked and Asa shielded Rowan and Indiga with her own body as pink shards flew into the crowd.

Indiga crumpled to the ground.

Chapter Twenty-Six:
DEFINE DISTRACTION

T he explosion echoed across the courtyard. *Boom!*
Fae screamed and ran for cover, their nightly rituals disturbed as fragments of rose quartz rained down in every direction. Windows shattered and vases broke. Some Fae even jumped into the reflecting pools to avoid being hit by stray shards of quartz.

Asa scooped an unconscious Indiga up and used the uproar to run toward the doors.

"What in Lucifer's name was that?" Dora yelled, hurrying toward the arched doorway.

"A distraction," Asa replied.

"Yeah, well next time we need to define the word *distraction* for Indiga. I thought she was supposed to just knock it down, not blow it up!"

"You are the one who said destruction follows her!" Asa said. She had to admit that this very crowded courtyard was in a state of pandemonium, which meant the distraction was a rousing success.

The doors cracked open, and they crept inside without anyone giving them a second glance.

"What was all the commotion? What happened to Indiga?" The mink rushed to the little Fae's side as Asa laid her down on the cool tourmaline floor. Indiga's golden curls fanned out around her. She resembled one of the sleeping princesses from the humans' fairy tales, but they were far from a happily-ever-after moment.

"She collapsed right after she blew up the obelisk," Asa said, placing her ear to the little Fae's chest.

"Blew up?" Holly clapped her paws against her head and turned to Rowan. "I said a distraction, not a war zone."

"Do not blame me, luv. Turns out she is quite the little powerhouse and overachiever. Blew the thing to bits." He did not attempt to conceal the pride in his voice.

"Is she going to be okay?" Asa's concern cut through the debate on Indiga's skill.

Dora crouched over Indiga's body to conduct a preliminary exam, touching pulse points. "She will be fine. Her aura is intact." She ran her hand up and down the center of the Little One's body, her palm hovering six inches above Indiga's heart. "Indiga was overwhelmed by the power surge. She will be unconscious for a few minutes, but her Chakras are equal, well ... as equal as they can be for Indiga. She released some pent-up frustration from her fifth Chakra. That is a good thing for her." Dora tucked her hand back inside her cloak and rose.

"'The healer becomes a leader,'" Rowan whispered to Holly, repeating a portion of the Oracle card prophecy. Holly nodded in response. "You are a healer?" Rowan inquired to confirm their hunch.

Dora gave him a quick half-smile and shook her head. "I am a simple tonic and tincture girl. I hope to be a healer one day for my faction. I will never be one like Lady Ambia—I am not of that bloodline—but, for now, I am an apprentice. I received my bracelets this last equinox." Dora pulled up her sleeves to show off the gold vine arm adornments. They started at her index finger, winding and twirling around each finger, then snaked around her wrist before they turned into perfect scarlet chrysanthemum blooms and continued up to her elbows. The gold vines glowed even in the darkness of the tunnels, as did the vibrant red petals of the flowers.

Holly brought her paw to her mouth, struck by the beauty of the cuffs. "What do they signify?" she asked, sniffing them. She examined the petals in wonder.

Dora smiled and straightened them. She was happy to explain her accomplishments. "I have been accepted by a teacher as their apprentice, and I am committed to the art of healing. The flowers represent my faction and remind me I am not to use my elemental connection. I vow to save life, not take it. The gold vines represent that I am bound to serve as a healer and that I must always be seeking knowledge, not worldly possessions. This will be the last gold I possess." Dora fixed the piece on her index finger, tightening it.

Rowan furrowed his brow. "What is your elemental connection?"

Dora's demeanor changed dramatically. Her back stiffened and she sucked in her cheeks. "E and I are cousins. He is gifted in ways I am not," she said, eager to end the conversation, but of course it did not.

Even as Dora tried to avoid the inquiries into her faction and elemental connection, Rowan and Holly pressed. They needed to know exactly what and with whom they were dealing, especially if they believed her to be the healer from the Oracles' prophecy card reading.

"That was not what I asked you, Dora," Holly said flatly.

Dora exhaled. She knew they were not about to let this go, and until Indiga woke up, they could not travel. "My father and E's mother were brother and sister. My parents were killed in the war very early on." Dora's gaze dropped, and she squared her shoulders. She had a spine with more steel in it than she had let on. "Aunt Eden, E's mother, took me in without question. However, E's father did not want me unless I signed on to take the path of a healer, because he knew the vow I would have to take." Holly and Rowan exchanged glances. "My faction is the Shedim. We are not fire conjurers. We control the element of Fire, but there are only a few who can use the elements around them to spark and combust. It is a rare gift in my faction, usually revered, and if a Fae is gifted with such control, they are uplifted to a minor House standing. Unless they are cursed with the Tempest Ignis."

Rowan's ears twitched, his bushy tail swaying. "It means 'their Fire,' if my Latin is correct. What is so bad about that?"

Dora shook her head and dropped her shoulders in a defeated manner, exhaling slowly. "There is no real translation for what it is to be a Tempest Ignis. Their fire, firestorm—it means your fire starts because of your emotions. The Tempest cannot control the fires they start since their emotions and element are intertwined. If they fall in love, a fire follows. If they are happy, there's a spark. Look out if you break a Tempest's heart—the entire village may burn to ash. These Fae have no restraint and are slaves to their element." The shame in her voice made it pointless to follow up with questions. "Uncle Narcissi made me ... I mean, had me sleep outside in a wading pool with Aunt Wendoura, my Mima, who kept watch over me so I would not drown. I slept like that until I was accepted onto the path. My nightmares caught the curtains on fire the first night I slept in his house. It was for the best."

Holly stroked Dora's back, but she shrugged her off.

"I do not deserve your kindness. I was a danger to my family. It is why I am to become a healer." She lifted her chin.

Holly sat in front of Dora, meeting her eyes. "You were a Little One! You suffered a great loss. You needed love and compassion, not isolation. Dora, do you even want to become a healer? It sounds like your uncle forced you to take this path."

Dora shook her head, her hands balling into fists. "Of course. It is the safest path for me. Uncle Narcissi was a very logical Fae. He wanted to keep his family safe. He wanted what was best for us. He kept us in line. He ran his house like he ran his armies. He was a revered strategist in the wars."

When he frowned, the fur around Rowan's mouth resembled a handlebar mustache. "Yeah, the bloke was something, all right." Holly stomped on his tail to keep him from saying anything else.

The mink should have trod on Asa's foot instead.

"Your uncle—E's father—is General Narcissi of the Azurite Faction?" Asa smoothed Indiga's hair back from her face and stood, glancing down at the little Fae one more time to make sure she was breathing evenly.

Suddenly filled with icy dread, Rowan eyed Holly.

Dora glanced up at the red-cloaked Fae. "You must have heard of him. He was considered a hero. He planned the ambush that took down several of the Dark Fae's ice dragons in the Secor Valley."

Rowan grumbled and licked his lips. He knew what was about to happen.

Chapter Twenty-Seven:
Simmer Down

"**I**s that what they told you?" Asa gave a derisive laugh. "That he devised an ingenious way to attack a bunch of defenseless spawning dragons? There was nothing inventive or clever about it, foolish Fae. General Narcissi ambushed the dragons in their sacred place of reproduction. If not for a few Dark Fae who sacrificed their lives defending those dragons, there might not be any Ice-Breathers left. Do not speak of how clever he was," Asa said, her words hot with disgust.

Dora stood. "My uncle did no such thing! The Dark Fae had their dragons lying in wait to attack the Undines at the River Ness. The Secor Valley runs counter to it in the Veil. He stopped them. We all know the Water Kelpie Grandmaster is a relative of the Draconians—he inhabits the Loch. Uncle Narcissi had information the Kelpies would aid the Dark Fae due to their relation to the dragons. He needed to make an example of the dragons."

Asa chuckled dryly. "No, that is not even remotely close to the truth. With the exception of the Water Kelpie

Grandmaster inhabiting Loch Ness and the Undines having territory in the surrounding River Ness, the rest is troll shit. Secor Valley is the spawning ground for the Ice-Breathers, and it was declared sacred by the Draconians. Every faction of Fae and animal have recognized it, except your uncle. The Water Kelpie Grandmaster had already stated he would remain neutral in the war. The Light Fae had no reason to fear him, but your uncle attacked the Water Kelpies, provoking them. He did it to get Queen Aurora to approve his plan. Most reasonable Fae realize Aurora did not know he attacked first, which was why she agreed to his plan in the first place. Had he not done that, the treaty would have been signed sooner; King Jarvok was in the process of agreeing to a negotiation. When Narcissi launched his attack against the Ice-Breathers, they were spawning on sacred ground. It was the one place, beside the Archway of Apala, where no blood was ever to be spilled. The Ice-Breathers trusted the Dark Fae to keep watch while the females laid their eggs. The Dark Fae set up guardposts around the dragons, but your uncle led his troops into the middle of their spawn while they were most vulnerable, contrary to the rules of engagement." Asa took a step forward, her index finger raised. "His troops killed many dragons while they were laying eggs and crushed the eggs of unborn dragons." She punched the air, punctuating her words. Her cheeks flushed with anger. "However, he and his troops were no match for the Dark Fae who stood watch, and when the night was over, the Dark prevailed. Yes, the Court of Dark lost dragons, but your uncle lost his entire army," Asa snarled. Triumph rang out in her voice.

Dora lifted her chin. "And how do you know? If there were no Light Fae survivors? You act like you were there." Her words were laced with sarcasm.

Nose to nose with Dora, Asa removed her hood and unsheathed her Elestial Blade, the soft white glow allowing Dora to see the scar of her Power Angel lineage. Dora gasped, but Asa was not finished. "Because I *was*, and I am the Dark Fae who delivered your uncle to his Oblivion that very day," she whispered through gritted teeth.

Rowan put his head down, sighing as his cheeks puffed out. "Well, so much for all of us getting along."

Epilogue

Hogal fumbled for the keys to his workshop, taking his time walking down the long hallway. The setting sun cast long shadows, and the corridor looked lonely, matching his mood. He felt like the color blue. Aurora was truly gone. He had seen her with his own eyes in the casket. Beautiful, even in Oblivion. Malascola and Theadova had asked him to go to the tavern for a drink of plum sugar wine to toast Aurora, but he had refused. Hogal wanted to be alone.

There was a loud boom in the distance, and the metal Gnome clutched at his heart. "Damns it to Lucifers," he exclaimed, dropping his keys. He bent down, listening to his knees creak and pop. Holding his back, he straightened. "Mes getting too old."

Hogal glanced around, trying to determine the origin of the sound, but eventually he gave up. "Must bes from the courtyard, theys started fighting again." He ambled to his workshop, still mumbling to himself. When he reached the entrance, he noticed a note pinned to the front door. It bore his name and was accompanied by a velvet pouch. The handwriting was not familiar to him. "What be this?" He grabbed the note and pouch and pushed inside his refuge.

Throwing his keys on his work bench, Hogal surveyed the room, specifically his shelf of crystals, and the pain of his loss returned tenfold. His lips trembled. How many times had he shown Aurora the projects on that shelf? He loved to give her a glimpse of what he would be making next and explain why he had chosen a specific crystal. He could never do it again. The tears fell like large raindrops. He wiped his cheek with the back of his hand.

Hogal tore open the note, still sniffling. It was from Desdemona:

Hogal,

I thought you would want this. I am checking on a few items that require my attention. However, I meant what I said in my quarters. I will take care of you. I hope you will see this as a token of my word.

We are each other's kin, which is what Aurora would have wanted.

~Desdemona

Hogal untied the laces on the pouch and turned it upside down. Aurora's sun and moon ring fell into his calloused palm. His mouth twisted; this was the first gift he had made for her as queen. He closed his fist around the ring, clutching it to his chest and kissing his knuckles. "Oh, mes queen," he whispered. He opened his hand to examine the ring; he remembered looking for the perfect moonstone, one that would reflect the right amount of opalescence. He had also thought himself so clever to include a secret compartment. Hogal flipped the moon and sun adornment up to see if Aurora had left a note. Only he and Aurora had known about the hidden compartment. *Maybe the note was in there,* he thought. To his sorrow, it was empty, much like his heart. But there was a secret.

Hogal's brow furrowed, creating more creases than the Gnome already had. "Whats in mes world?" He pulled out a lock of auburn hair. Hogal held it in his thumb and index finger, examining it. It was fine, clearly belonging to an infant. He clamped his hand over his mouth and raced to lock his door. He hid the hair back inside the ring. Hogal looked around his workshop. "Nos plants, Hogal," he chided himself. He checked the rest of the shop, making sure there was no plant life. Then he went to a large boulder sitting in the corner of his workshop.

Hogal braced his feet and outstretched his right hand, and the boulder cracked and slid open, leaving scratches on the floor. The inside was raw amethyst, with glittering points of purple in shades ranging from eggplant to lavender. Hogal gently placed the ring inside. He stepped back, and with his closed fist gave the command for the boulder to snap shut, protecting the ring.

The Gnome stumbled back and found a stool to support himself. He took his red beanie off and tossed it on his work bench before running his hands through his wiry white hair. He breathed heavily from the strain of his elemental Magick and the weight of his discovery.

"Mes queen hads a babe with Jarvok! Thats be why she was actings outs of sorts. This was to bes protecting the babe. Oh, Aurora." He cried from surprise and loss.

"Do the Dark Faes King knows?" Hogal shook his head. "No, if he be knowings, Jarvoks wouldn't have dones this.

Mes queen didn't tell hims." Hogal lifted his head, and the room became very cold. "The bishops knew."

Geddes had taken an interest in Hogal's work just before Aurora's death, always asking if he was working on any new projects for the queen. The bishop had even asked if Hogal was doing any woodworking, which at the time the Gnome had thought was odd, but now he understood they had wanted to know if he was making a cradle. Geddes was checking to see how much Hogal knew.

"Geddes was going to tries to sends mes to my Oblivion. Lets hims try. Bigs ol' boulder. I control Earth. They forgets mes lived with the crystals of the earth."

Hogal wondered if Desdemona knew too. He glanced at the boulder. If Aurora had a child, they had a claim to the throne, not Sekhmet. "Ooh, things goings to get sticky 'round here!"

Wow! Secrets are running rampant in the Veil! Looks like Indiga was correct about the oversized butterfly too. I hope you enjoyed *Birth of the Fae: A Fae Is Done*. Indiga, Dora, Asa, Rowan, and Holly will return in Book Six, *Birth of the Fae: Forgive Us*. Many more adventures await the Fae, as this journey is far from over. Will Asa and the Little Ones rescue E? First, they have to deal with the issue of Asa killing General Narcissi! Will Queen Sekhmet prove to be a righteous ruler, or will Desdemona have to put her oath to the ultimate test? Let me know your thoughts on Instagram @Birthofthefae_novel or on Twitter @Birthofthefae. Stay up to date on all things Fae at Birthofthefae.com, and make sure you subscribe to my newsletter to be the first to read preview chapters from upcoming books.

~Chaos be with you,
Danielle

4 Horsemen Publications

Romance

Ann Shepphird
The War Council

Emily Bunney
All or Nothing
All the Way
All Night Long: Novella
All She Needs
Having it All
All at Once
All Together
All for Her

Lynn Chantale
The Baker's Touch
Blind Secrets
Broken Lens

Mimi Francis
Private Lives
Private Protection
Run Away Home
The Professor

Fantasy, SciFi, & Paranormal Romance

Beau Lake
The Beast Beside Me
The Beast Within Me
Taming the Beast: Novella
The Beast After Me
Charming the Beast: Novella
The Beast Like Me
An Eye for Emeralds
Swimming in Sapphires
Pining for Pearls

D. Lambert
To Walk into the Sands
Rydan
Celebrant
Northlander
Esparan

King
Traitor
His Last Name

J.M. Paquette
Klauden's Ring
Solyn's Body
The Inbetween
Hannah's Heart
Call Me Forth
Invite Me In
Keep Me Close

Lyra R. Saenz
Prelude
Falsetto in the Woods: Novella

Ragtime Swing
Sonata
Song of the Sea
The Devil's Trill
Bercuese
To Heal a Songbird
Ghost March
Nocturne

T.S. Simons
Antipodes
The Liminal Space
Ouroboros
Caim

Sessrúmnir

Valerie Willis
Cedric: The Demonic Knight
Romasanta: Father of
Werewolves
The Oracle: Keeper of the
Gaea's Gate
Artemis: Eye of Gaea
King Incubus: A New Reign

V.C. Willis
Prince's Priest
Priest's Assassin

Young Adult Fantasy

Blaise Ramsay
Through The Black Mirror
The City of Nightmares
The Astral Tower
The Lost Book of the Old Blood
Shadow of the Dark Witch
Chamber of the Dead God

C.R. Rice
Denial
Anger
Bargaining
Depression
Acceptance

Broken Beginnings:
Story of Thane
Shattered Start: Story of Sera
Sins of The Father:
Story of Silas
Honorable Darkness: Story of
Hex and Snip
A Love Lost: Story of Radnar

Valerie Willis
Rebirth
Judgment
Death

4HorsemenPublications.com